Doris Virginia Taylor

Room 205A

TENDER
SHOOTS

PAUL MORAND

TENDER
SHOOTS

Translated from the French by
Euan Cameron

PUSHKIN PRESS
LONDON

Pushkin Press
71-75 Shelton Street
London WC2H 9JQ

Original text © Éditions Gallimard
English translation © Euan Cameron 2011
Afterword © Michel Déon 2011

Tender Shoots first published in French as
Tendres Stocks in 1921.

First published by Pushkin Press in 2011
Reprinted in 2012

ISBN 978 1 906548 65 0

Cover Illustration: *Three Women* Marie Laurencin
© ADAGP Paris and DACS London 2011

Frontispiece Paul Morand 1935
© Roger-Violet Rex Features

Set in 11 on 14 Monotype Baskerville by Tetragon
Proudly printed and bound in Great Britain
by TJ International, Padstow, Cornwall
on Munken Premium White 90gsm

www.pushkinpress.com

CONTENTS

PREFACE

Marcel Proust

T HE ATHENIANS ARE SLOW to deliver. So far, only three young ladies or gentlewomen have been given up to our minotaur Morand, and the treaty allows for seven. But the year is not yet ended. And many undisclosed postulants seek the glorious fate of Clarissa and Aurora. I should have liked to undertake the unnecessary task of composing a fitting preface for the charming novellas that bear the names of these fair creatures. But an unforeseen occurrence has prevented me from doing so. A stranger has chosen to make her home in my brain. She came and she went; before long, having observed the way she behaved, I came to know her habits. Furthermore, like an over-attentive lodger, she tried to strike up a personal relationship with me. I was surprised to discover that she was not beautiful. For I had always supposed Death so to be. Otherwise, how would she get the better of us? Be that as it may, she seems to have gone away today. Probably not for long, to judge by all she has left behind. And it would be more sensible to take advantage of the respite she allows me other than by writing a preface for an author who is already well known and has no need of one.

Another consideration should have deterred me. My dear master Anatole France, whom I have not seen, alas, for more than twenty years, has recently written an article for the *Revue de Paris* in which he asserts that all distinctiveness in style should be rejected. Now, it is certain that Paul Morand's style is distinctive. Were I to have the pleasure once more of seeing M France, whose kindnesses to me are alive in my memory, I would ask him how he can believe in a uniformity of style, given that our sensibilities are distinctive. Stylistic beauty is indeed the infallible sign that the mind has become exalted, that it has discovered and established the necessary links between objects whose contingency had separated them. In *Le Crime de Sylvestre Bonnard*, does not the twofold impression of wildness and sweetness provided by the cats radiate within an admirable passage: "Hamilcar, I said to him as I stretched out my legs, sleepy prince of the citadel of books ... (I do not have the book to hand). In this citadel protected by the military virtues, sleep with the softness of a sultan's wife. For you combine the formidable aspect of a Tartar warrior with the heavy grace of women from the East. Heroic, voluptuous Hamilcar … " and so on. But M France would not agree with me that this passage is admirable, for people have written badly ever since the end of the eighteenth century.

People have written badly ever since the end of the eighteenth century. In truth, here is something that could give much food for thought. There can be no doubt that many authors wrote badly in the nineteenth century. When M France asks us to relinquish Guizot and Thiers to him (a rapprochement that does great dishonour to Guizot) we happily obey him, and, without waiting for other names to be summoned forth, of our own accord we toss him all the Villemains and Cousins that he could wish. M Taine, with his prose as variegated as a relief map, so as to more keenly impress pupils in secondary schools, might receive some recognition but be banished nonetheless. If, for his legitimate expression of moral truths, we were to retain M Renan, we would still have to admit that he sometimes writes extremely badly. Without mentioning his recent works, in which the colour is so constantly out of focus that a comic effect seems to have been sought by the author, nor his very earliest work, littered with exclamation marks and with the constant over-exuberance of a choirboy, his fine *Origines du christianisme* is for the most part badly written. Rarely in a prose writer of outstanding ability does one encounter such pictorial impotence. The description of Jerusalem, the first time that Jesus arrives there, is composed in the style of Baedeker: "The buildings vie with the most perfect achievements of Antiquity in their grandiose character, the perfection of execution and the beauty of the materials. A number of superb tombs, of original taste … " And yet this was a 'passage' that was to be particularly 'cherished'. And Renan felt obliged to invest all his passages with a pomposity very much in the Ary Scheffer, Gounod manner (we might add César Franck had he written nothing but the solemn, affected intermezzo of his *Redemption*). In order to give a dignified ending to a book or a preface, he uses those dutiful schoolboy images that are certainly not formed by any impression. "Now the apostolic bark will be able to fill its sails." "When the overwhelming light had given way to the countless army of stars." "Death struck us both with its wing." And yet during those visits to Jerusalem, when M

Renan calls him a "young Jewish democrat", and speaks of the "naiveties" that fell "incessantly" from this "provincial" (how like Balzac!) one wonders, as I once allowed myself to do, whether, while fully recognising Renan's genius, the *Vie de Jésus* is not a sort of Belle Hélène of Christianity. But M France shall not triumph quite so easily. As for our ideas about style, we will let him know some other time. But is he quite certain that the nineteenth century is lacking in this regard?

There is often something objective and incisive about Baudelaire's style, but as far as power alone is concerned, has it ever been equalled? Surely no one has written anything less charitable, yet at the same time so forceful, as his lines on Charity:

> *A raging angel swoops from heaven like an eagle*
> *He grasps the infidel's hair in his fist*
> *And, shaking him, says: "You shall know the rule!*
> *[...]*
> *Know that you must love, without contemptuous face,*
> *The poor, the wicked, the tortured, the simpleton,*
> *So that when Jesus passes you may make*
> *A triumphal carpet with your charity."*

Nor anything more sublime but less expressive of the essence of devout souls than:

> *They say to Devotion who lent them his wings—*
> *Mighty hippogryph, carry me to heaven.*

Besides, Baudelaire is a great classic poet and, strangely enough, this classicism of form increases in proportion to the licence of his depictions. Racine may have written more profound verses, but with no greater purity of style than that of the sublime *Poèmes condamnés*. In the poem that caused the greatest scandal:

> *Her vanquished arms, cast down like futile weapons,*
> *All served, all adorned her fragile beauty.*

might have been taken from *Britannicus*.

Poor Baudelaire! After begging for an article from Sainte-Beuve (with what tenderness, what deference!), all he receives are tributes such as: "What is certain is that M Baudelaire *benefits from being seen*. Just when you expect a strange, eccentric man to enter the room, you find yourself in the presence of a polite, respectful, kindly young man, well spoken and wholly conventional in appearance." So as to thank him for his dedication in *Les Fleurs du mal*, the only compliment that Sainte-Beuve can bring himself to offer is that the effect of these poems when collected together is altogether different. He goes on to pick out a few poems to which he applies double-edged epithets, such as "precious" and "subtle", and asks: "But why were they not written in Latin, or rather in Greek?" A fine tribute to French poetry! Baudelaire's relationship with Sainte-Beuve (whose stupidity is so obvious that one wonders whether it is not feigned so as to mask his cowardice) is one of the most distressing and at the same time comical episodes in French literature. For a time I wondered whether M Daniel Halévy was not making fun of me when, in a splendid article in *La Minerve française*, he attempted to gain my sympathy for Sainte-Beuve's unctuous remarks, addressing Baudelaire with crocodile tears: "My poor child, how you must have suffered." By way of thanks, Sainte-Beuve said to Baudelaire: "I've a good mind to scold you … you single out, you Petrarchise what is horrible. And (I quote from memory) one day when we are walking together by the seashore, I should like to trip you up, and force you to swim in the full current." We must not pay too much attention to the image itself (which is likely to be better in its context), for Sainte-Beuve, who knew nothing at all about such things, took his imagery from the hunting field, from marine life, etc. He would say: "I should like to take a blunderbuss and march off into the middle of nowhere to fire off at will." He would say of a book: "It's an etching", though he would not have been capable of recognising an etching. But he reckoned that in a literary way it struck the right note, and was dainty and graceful. But how could M Daniel Halévy (in the twenty-five years since I last saw him, he has continued to grow in authority) seriously think that rather than it being this crafty jumbler of phrases who "singles out and Petrarchises", it is to the great genius that we owe (lines that are not in the least "singled out" and seem to me to be in "full current"):

> *For the child in love with maps and prints*
> *The Universe is equal to his huge appetite.*
> *How vast is the world by lamplight!*
> *How small is the world in memory's eyes!*

Worse still, when Baudelaire was prosecuted on account of *Les Fleurs du mal*, Sainte-Beuve refused to testify on his behalf, but wrote him a letter which he immediately asked to be returned to him once he realised that it was intended to make it public. When he published it later in his *Causeries du lundi*, he felt it was his duty to preface it with a short preamble (which would have the effect of making it feebler still) in which he stated that this letter was written "with the thought of coming to the aid of the defence". The accolade was scarcely compromising, however. "The poet Baudelaire (it was said) had spent years extracting from every subject, and from every flower, an essence that was poisonous, and even, one has to say, pleasantly poisonous. He was furthermore a witty man, fairly likeable, and, at times, very capable of affection. When he published this collection entitled *Les Fleurs du mal*, he was not merely dealing with his critics, justice was involved too, as if there really was danger in these disguised pranks, and hidden meaning in the elegant rhyming" (which, incidentally, hardly tallies with "My poor child, how you must have suffered"). What is more, in this scheme for his own defence, Sainte-Beuve speaks well of an illustrious poet ("far be it from me to detract in any way from the fame of an illustrious poet, of a poet dear to us all, whom the Emperor has deemed worthy of a public funeral"). Unfortunately, this poet who is ultimately glorified is not Baudelaire, but Béranger. When Baudelaire, on the advice of Sainte-Beuve, withdraws his candidature for the Académie, the great critic congratulates him, and believes he has filled his cup with joy by telling him: "When they read your final sentence of thanks, written in such modest and courteous terms, they said aloud: 'Very good'." The most alarming thing is that not only does Sainte-Beuve think that he has behaved very well towards Baudelaire, but, alas, that in the appalling lack of encouragement, or simple justice, accorded Baudelaire, the poet shares the critic's opinion and literally does not know how to express his gratitude to him.

However enthralling this story of a genius who underestimated himself may be, we must tear ourselves away and return to the matter of style. It certainly did not have the same importance for Stendhal as it did for Baudelaire. When Beyle described a landscape as "these enchanting spots", "these beautiful places", and wrote of one of his heroines as "this admirable woman", he did not wish to be any more specific. He was so unspecific that he could allow himself to write: "She wrote him an interminable letter." But if we consider that vast unconscious framework that encompasses the desired structure of ideas as being an aspect of style, then Stendhal has it. How much pleasure it would give me to show that each time Julien Sorel or Fabrice leave behind their vain cares to live a selfless and pleasure-seeking life, they always find themselves in some elevated place (be it Fabrice's prison, or Julien's, in the Abbé Banès's observatory). This is as beautiful as those homage-bearing creatures, rather similar to latter-day Angels who, here and there, in Dostoevsky's work, bow down low at the feet of the one they imagine they have slaughtered.

Thus, Beyle was a great writer without being conscious of the fact. He ranked literature not merely lower than life, when, on the contrary, it is the goal, but beneath its dreariest distractions. I confess that, were it sincere, nothing would shock me more than this passage from Stendhal: "Some people arrived and we did not part until very late. The nephew ordered an excellent zambajon from the Café Pedroti. In the country where I am going, I said to my friends, I am unlikely to find a household such as this, and to pass the long evening hours, I shall write a novel about our kind Duchess Sanseverina." *La Chartreuse de Parme*, written for lack of a household where there is pleasant conversation and where they serve zambajon, there you have the complete antithesis of the poem or even the one-line alexandrine, towards which, according to Mallarmé, the various and fruitless activities of universal life all aim.

"Since the end of the eighteenth century no one has known how to write." Would not the converse be just as true? In every art form, it would appear that talent is a bringing together of the artist and the object that is to be expressed. As long as the gulf remains, the job is not finished. A violinist may play his solo part very well, but you can see the effect; you applaud, he is a virtuoso. When all that has eventually vanished, when the violinist's phrasing is of one being with the artist, then the miracle will have been accomplished. In other centuries, it seems as if there had always been a certain distance between the object and the lofty minds that deliberated about it. But with Flaubert, for instance, his intellect, which may not have been among the greatest, strives to become the vibration of a steamship, the colour of the foam, an island in the bay. There then comes a point when we no longer see this intellect (even Flaubert's moderate intellect), and we have before us the boat that sails on "encountering trails of logs that began to toss about in the waves made by the wash". This tossing about is intellect transformed, mind that has integrated with matter. It also manages to penetrate the moors, the beech trees, the silence and the light of the undergrowth. This transformation of energy, in which the thinker has disappeared and trails things before us, is this not the writer's first attempt at style?

But M France does not agree. "What is your canon?" he asks us in this article that launches André Chaumeix's new *Revue de Paris* with such a splash. And among those he puts forward, and compared to whom we write badly, he mentions Racine's *Lettres aux imaginaires*. We reject the very principle of a 'canon', which would imply a uniform style independent of the many aspects of thinking. But if we actually had to choose one, and one which in M France's terms might be considered "heavy artillery", we would never choose the *Lettres aux imaginaires*. Nothing so dry, so impoverished, so slender. It is not difficult for a form that embodies so little thought to be light and graceful. Yet that of the *Lettres aux imaginaires* is neither: "I would even go so far as to say that you are not from Port Royal as one of you claims … How many people have read his letter who *would not have* looked at it *had* Port Royal not approved of it, *had* not these gentlemen distributed it … " etc. "You believe you are *saying* something extremely agreeable, for instance, when you *say* of a remark made by M Chamillard, that his capital O is merely the number 0 … it is quite clear that you are doing your utmost to *be* pleasant. But this is not the way to *be* so." These repetitions would certainly not have interrupted the flow of a sentence by Saint-Simon, but where is the flow here, where the poetry, or even the style? These letters to the author of *Les Imaginaires* are almost as feeble as the absurd correspondence in which Racine and Boileau exchange their medical views. Very little that is medical. Boileau's snobbishness (or rather what would nowadays be the excessive deference of a functionary towards officialdom) is such that he prefers the opinion of Louis XIV (who was wise enough not to give it) to consultations with doctors. He was convinced that a prince who had succeeded in capturing Luxembourg must be "inspired by Heaven" and could not utter more than "oracles" even in medicine. (I feel sure that in their entirely justified admiration for the Duc d'Orléans, my masters M Léon Daudet and M Charles Maurras, and their charming disciple Jacques Bainville, would not go so far as to ask him for medical advice from afar.) Furthermore, Boileau adds, who would not be happy to "lose his voice and even his tongue" on discovering that the King had asked for news of him?

Let it not be said that this has to do with a particular period, and that at that time epistolary style was always like this. Without looking very far, on a certain Wednesday in 1673 (in December, as far as we know), that is to say just in between the *Imaginaires* in 1666 and the *Lettres* of Racine and Boileau in 1687, Mme de Sévigné wrote from Marseilles: "I am charmed by the singular beauty of this city. Yesterday, the weather was divine, and the place from which I overlooked the sea, the farmhouses, the mountains and the town is astonishing. The throng of noblemen who came to see M de Grignan yesterday; well-known names,

Saint-Hérems etc.; adventurers, swords, fashionable
hats; people born to depict an idea of war, of ro-
mance, of embarkation, of adventure, of chains, of
slaves' shackles, of servitude, of captivity: I, who love
romances, was delighted by it all." Admittedly, this is
not one of those letters by Mme de Sévigné that I like
best. Nevertheless, in its composition, its colouring, its
variety, what a picture for a "French gallery" in the
Louvre this great writer succeeded in painting. Such
as it is, in its splendour, I dedicate it to a member of
the family to which Mme de Sévigné (she never stops
saying this) was so proud to be related through the
Grignans, to my friend the Marquis de Castellane.

Compared to such passages, the meagre correspondence we were discussing matters little. This does mean
to say, of course, that Boileau was not an excellent,
sometimes delightful, poet. And no doubt a hysterical
genius was struggling in Racine's mind, kept in check
by a superior intellect, and in his tragedies it simulated
for him, with a perfection that has never been equalled,
the flux and reflux, the pitching and the tossing, fully
grasped nevertheless, of passion. But all the admissions
(withdrawn the moment they are felt to have been
badly received, and reiterated, if it is feared, despite all

evidence to the contrary, that they may not have been understood, and then, after many a tortuous detour, fanned into a raging blaze) that so inimitably enliven any scene from *Phèdre* cannot prevent us, retroactively, from feeling surprised and not remotely charmed by the *Lettres aux imaginaires*. Were we bound absolutely to adopt a canon of the kind that can be extracted from these *Lettres*, we should much prefer, at a time when, if we are to believe M. France, people no longer knew how to write, the preface (to do with his moods of near-insanity) that Gérard de Nerval dedicated to Alexandre Dumas: "They [his sonnets] would lose their charm by being explained, if that were possible; grant me credit at least for expressing myself; the last folly that will probably remain to me is to think of myself as a poet—it is up to the critics to cure me of it." Here, if we are to take the *Imaginaires* as a canon, is something that is well written, that is much better written. But we do not want a "canon" of any sort. The truth is (and M France knows this better than anyone for he knows everything better than anyone else) that from time to time a new and original writer emerges (let us call him, if you will, Jean Giraudoux or Paul Morand, since, I cannot think why, Morand and Giraudoux are always being compared to each other, just as Natoire and Falconet are in the marvellous *Nuit à Châteauroux*, without their bearing any resemblance to one another). This new writer is generally fairly tiring to read and hard to understand because he brings things together through new relationships. We follow him easily through the first half of the sentence, but there we flag. And we feel that this is only because the new writer is nimbler than us. Original writers spring up just as original painters do. When Renoir began to paint, people did not recognise the things he depicted. Nowadays it is easy to say he was an eighteenth-century painter. But, in saying this, we omit the temporal factor, and that it took a long time, even well into the nineteenth century, for Renoir to be recognised as a great artist. To succeed, the original painter, the original writer, proceed in the way oculists do. The treatment—whether in their painting, their writing—is not always pleasant. When it is over, they tell us: "Now look". And suddenly the world, which has not been created only once, but is recreated as often as a new artist emerges, appears to us—so different from the old world—in perfect clarity. We adore Renoir's, Morand's or Giraudoux's women, whereas before they were given this treatment, we refused to see them as women. And we feel a need to walk in the forest that at first sight had seemed to us to be anything but a forest, and more, for example, like a tapestry of a thousand shades of colour in which the actual tints of the forests were lacking. Such is the new and perishable universe which the artist creates, and which will endure until a new one surfaces. To all of which there may be many things to add. But the reader, who has already guessed what they are, will be able to explain them, better than I could, by reading *Clarissa*, *Aurora* and *Delphine*.

The only criticism I might be tempted to suggest to Morand is that he sometimes uses imagery other than the inevitable images. Now, all approximate images do not count. Water (given certain conditions) boils at one hundred degrees. At ninety-eight, at ninety-nine, the phenomenon does not occur. Therefore, better not to have any images. Put someone who knows neither Wagner nor Beethoven in front of a piano for six months and let him try out every combination of notes on the keys that happen to occur to him, never from out of this jumble of notes will he give birth to the Spring theme in *Die Walküre* or the pre-Mendelssohnian (or rather infinitely super-Mendelssohnian) phrase of the Fifteenth Quartet. It is the same criticism that might have been levelled at Péguy while he was alive, of trying to say something in ten different ways, when there is only one. The glory of his admirable death has expunged everything.

It seems as if hitherto it has been in French and foreign mansions, built by architects inferior to Daedalus, that our minotaur Morand has sought the meanderings of his "vast retreat", as Phèdre calls it in the scene to which I have just alluded. There he lies in wait for the young girls in their gowns, their sleeves fluttering like wings, who have been unwise enough to descend into the Labyrinth. I do not know these mansions any better than he does and would be of no use to him "in unwinding the uncertain predicament". But if, before he becomes an Ambassador and competes with Consul Beyle, he wishes to visit the Hôtel de Balbec, then I will offer him the fatal thread.

C'est moi, prince, c'est moi dont l'utile secours
Vous a du labyrinthe enseigné les détours.*

---

* *'Tis I, prince, 'tis I whose valuable assistance/Has taught you the winding path out of the labyrinth.*

CLARISSA

To the memory of E B

I KNEW YOU, Clarissa, in happy days. Those days, filled so easily with our petty cares, recalled your glass cabinets, too narrow to contain the thousand pointless and precious knick-knacks that you loved. We used to meet every night in the best lit, most sonorous houses in town, where we would dance. Sleep would later carry me far into the day and often the ringing of the telephone would wake me up:

"Look out of the window," you would say, "I am sending you a beautiful cloud!"

I scarcely had time to put down the receiver (for our houses were next door to one another), I ran barefoot to the window and I saw coming towards me, trailing across the sky, the pink or grey mass you had told me about, heavy and as if weighed down with the welcome it brought me.

I would go and collect you in a great hurry—for these winter afternoons are short—to haggle over a piece of silk, yet another useless item, at some antique dealer's in Ebury Street where we arrived late, while across the shop floor already wreathed in shadow a last glimmer of light shone on the gold of the lacquers, on the steel of the weapons and on the false teeth of the antique dealer who amused you.

Those were happy days.

When I immerse myself in their memory, two visions loom up.

It is nighttime; a clear night, one of very few in a rain-filled spring whose warm, blue humidity it continues to exhale. The windows are open; we are standing on the balcony, our elbows on the parapet. You are leaning over to breathe in the smell of the newly mown grass that wafts up from Kensington and mingles with the animal perfume of the dance; the green acid of your Longhi cloak hangs down over the bright orange colour of the hump-backed Japanese bridge; pressed against the railings by the masks is a woman with bare breasts who laughs as she tosses bread to the carp. While the Venetian *Bauta* mask sets your face in shadow, allowing only a curious chemical-red mouth to be seen, the night girds all this feasting in a rich, velvety shade, illuminated only by the upturned wheels of the big dipper, which tumbles vertically above us in a motionless fall.

Now it is daytime, in the countryside.

The tennis court seems to have been cut into the truncated hilltop, from where the county rolls down to the sea in gentle undulations, like sumptuous, unused parkland. A young man dressed in whites accompanies the ball which he tosses up, and which his opponent is expecting, in an elongated action, gathering his movements and his shadow around him. On a mound of blue grass some young women dressed in cherry, yellow, green, cherry jumpers gather around the tea, which is served on a rattan table. And the centre of all brightness, of this glistening jollity, the luminous axle of this circle of women who are surrounded in turn by the still vaster ring of countryside and sky, is the silver teapot which sings like the wasps on the tart—reflected in the lid is a convex image of the sky, the shadow of the trees; in its ribbed body, the attenuated shapes of the figures, and, in narrow streaks, the jumpers, cherry, yellow, green, cherry.

But how can one detach oneself for a single second from the present moment?

Here is a muddy moor where the sparse grass oozes like a sponge, over which the rotting green light of dusk falls; nothing restricts it except the sky and, to the left, the white wooden shacks from which the smell of rancid butter reaches my nostrils. In the puddles of water the image of an aluminium moon sends back its reflection into the washed sky, emptied of its rain. On the disintegrating roads, the faceted wheels of heavy artillery create vertebrate potholes filled with mauve water.

Then up the steep-sided road that connects the arsenal to the barracks, climb soldiers in battledress. In the mud, beneath the low sky, ammunition wagons sway, drawn by brewers' horses, driven by soldiers with gentle, inscrutable faces. Behind them, the plain runs down towards the leaden river, covered as far as the eye can see with tents, wagons, naval guns without mounts, shaken apart with layers of violet earth, as regular as mole-hills, the trenches of the New Army.

Lastly, set against the sky is the city with its rearing chimneys, its squat gasometers, the lattice-girder railway bridges, the shiny rails, the signal discs, the masts of the sailing ships, the heavy smoke of the vessels under steam, and the arsenal dipping its pink steps in the river's rising tide.

You did not believe in the war. You used to say:

"Anyway, it won't last long."

"It would be too awful … "

Or:

"It's impossible, I've been to Munich."

But the Germans made war on France in order to be able to come to the Café de Paris in uniform. They made war on England because they were convinced that English tailors made badly cut clothes for them deliberately.

When I telephoned to tell you that Germany had declared war on Russia, you replied:

"I was in the garden, I was cutting some roses … "

You were upset thinking about all your relatives, your friends of France, but you could not rid yourself of that sense of security of those who live in a place surrounded by water.

This country awoke slowly to the war. The evidence came from outside, on seeing the German Jews from Commercial Road closing their shutters, those from the West End hiding away their pictures, the slump of consols in London, the collapse of wool in Sydney, the Americans fleeing in their nickel-plated motorcars, and gold, more fearful still; on hearing that arthritic diplomats were leaving the spas, that kings were returning to their capitals, that other countries were closing their frontiers like bolted doors. Then it was the departure of the French hairdressers and chefs, going down to the stations carrying a flag.

Warships could be seen sailing from Portsmouth as they did every year, for the regattas, but the stoppers had been removed from their guns and the German yachts did not come. The sea reacted first, then the coasts where the coastguard reservists climbed up to the semaphores with their kit folded inside a green canvas bag. And the fever eventually spread from the edges to the centre.

All this took place imperceptibly. England did not experience that sleepless August night when millions of men kissed their wives with dry lips and burned their letters. She paid no attention to the commotion, did not close her portholes, did not slip her moorings.

Just one policeman was put on duty outside the German embassy.

And when they realised, some barracks were built.

But could it be realised other than slowly, in this unscarred country, where children have never discovered cannonballs from previous wars embedded in the walls of houses?

Would you hope to see at a given signal the streets empty themselves of their cars, of their passers-by? The lawyers in gowns, the ushers in amaranthine robes, the judges in wigs, the bookmakers in putty-coloured overcoats with mother-of-pearl buttons, setting out on foot to the railway stations, making their way to the inland garrisons, and the peers keeping watch on the bridges over which no packed trains were yet passing, towards our frontier?

I hear you coming, Clarissa. You walk on your heels, with big, decisive footsteps; your dress makes no silken rustling noise; you are whistling a ragtime tune.

You are tall, broad-shouldered; a lovely figure and red hair. You are not vain about your beauty, but you like to draw attention to your hair.

You say:

"I adore redheads. As soon as a redhead appears anywhere, I notice her."

You loathe the indirect compliments that dark-haired women aspire to, affirming hypocritically that only blondes know how to please; you say:

"I'm a redhead. Like all redheads, I'm bad-tempered."

At first, you are not pleasant, especially when someone meets you socially for the first time, without your house, without your friends, without all that explains you, with a hat and gloves. You glance around you disdainfully, you purse your lips, you hold your head high and you seem to be saying to people:

"I'm taller than you."

You are so badly dressed! Yet in the very best taste. Your shoes are pointed at the toe; one expects to see flat heels; your dresses are simple, short, with pockets; you wear them for a very long time and from morning till evening. One imagines that your toilette is complete once you get out of the bath, when you are clean. Rising at seven o'clock, you come down to breakfast at eight, fully dressed. You have stray wisps of hair and you tuck them under your hat with your finger, in the motorcar.

When I criticise you, you reply:

"I haven't the time. There are more interesting things to do."

This indifference is not a pose, for one sometimes finds you making concessions to fashion (especially in evening dresses), and one is sorry you should have made them.

You are not unaware, however, of what people wear, since you yourself design for others what should be worn, and you like the company of eccentrically attired women and well dressed young men.

I have sometimes succeeded in making you discard dresses that are fifteen years out of date for those of thirty years ago. And when you want to please me, you arrange your hair in a fringe, and you wear a black velvet ribbon around your neck, "*à la Dégas*".

From the first day I was extremely curious about you, and I have remained so. Only your rebellious character has prevented me from loving you.

Your face is interesting. There is a great mystery in your taut lips, a great deal of sensuality in your nose with its restless, broad nostrils, and attractiveness in your yellow eyes, hypersensitive, generally rather hard, listless at times, and restricted at the corners by a mauve vein.

Without being well-educated, you know a great deal. You know nothing about history, but you know the past and you understand it better than a scholar, when you hold a piece of embroidery, or an old slipper, in your hands.

You do not like books. I have never seen you read a novel. In your library there are only pictures, documents and catalogues.

I know you will never grow old, will never end. When I feel like dying, I come and call on you when you are getting ready. You do not stop what you are doing, but as you continue to polish your nails or lace up your boots, you exclaim:

"Live! Tell yourself: 'I'm alive', my friend, and that's all you need! To be able to run, stop, to be in good form, to feel weary, to be able to spit, to spit in the fire, in the water, spit out of your window on the heads of passers-by, how good and wonderful all that is!"

And you really are like that—you rejoice in your good health, in the beating of your pulse, in the use of your limbs, in all these good fortunes, which for us are negative, with lucidity; when you wave your arms about, you experience the pleasure one would feel knowing there is only one hour left before they are to be amputated; when you use your legs, the joy of a paralytic who is suddenly able to move again. You take possession of a room, of a pavement, as if they had long been forbidden to you. You give the singular impression of a people's feast-day when the crowds, pressed into the clutch of run-down streets, spill out over the grass like laundry.

Life is so much a part of you that one would have to be very determined to take it away from you. Dentists do their very best and cannot even manage to loosen one of your teeth. You pay no heed to illness. You stand up to English doctors.

I find Clarissa in her drawing room, her hands and face black, her clothing covered in dust.

"I'm tidying up," she says.

Clarissa claims to like open spaces, bare walls, polished floors in which they are prolonged, clear tables. But she succumbs, a victim of her liking for trinkets; she yields to successive solicitations of form, colour, feeling, and soon the glass cabinets, the occasional tables, the mantelpiece, are not enough; without her realising, the knick-knacks pile up in wooden chests, beneath the furniture; the drawers will no longer close, even access to the room becomes improbable. One day, Clarissa reacts; in sorrowful severance, she tears herself away from all these beloved trifles, banishes them to the attic where, having forgotten them, she discovers them years later and puts them back in their place, for the time being.

All day, she roams around the suburban antique dealers, the second-hand shops of the Hebrew districts, the clothes vendors. Basket in hand, she sets off, with her long strides, to the scrap merchants and, unconcerned about fleas, approaches the dealers, rummages around with her rag-and-bone man's instinct and returns home, her pockets and muff laden with new trinkets. She accommodates them all, from the rarest object to screws, doorknobs, nails, old coins.

"I'm like a magpie," she says.

And like a magpie, she pounces on shiny objects and buries them away in hiding-places that she alone knows, jumbled up with other things found in the street. When will they be put on display, Clarissa?

Her bedroom is full of coloured goblets, of bits of broken glass, of decanter stoppers, of crystal-ware, of fragments of chandeliers or mirrors, of spun-glass animals.

"How lovely it is to touch all these!"

And she runs her fingers over the corners, the surfaces and, going over to the window, she holds them against the light, rejoicing in their reflections. From the pavement, you can recognise her balcony by some crystal globes; from her ceiling she hangs glass balls in which the entire street's truncated and multifaceted images are reflected, in which the clouds swirl, slowly, the buses, rapidly.

Clarissa keeps up with the sales rooms, all the sales rooms, assiduously.

In London, there is no one large market through which everything that is for sale passes from hand to hand, but a series of auction houses, each with its distinct appearance, its customs, its own clientele. It is more than a difference of neighbourhood, a social hierarchy. But Clarissa sees it merely as a short or a long trip to be made from one to the other.

First she will go to the pretentious sales rooms, with monumental staircases, with liveried porters, where they deal with museum pieces, with precious goods forfeited by royalty, with large inheritances, under the watchful gaze of ennobled experts, of titled critics.

Just around the corner, it will be a caricature of these same rooms—the same porters, but older, their livery threadbare; exhibitions of unknown grand masters, brazen Rembrandts, indecent Corots, sold to a gang of shifty dealers and racketeers.

Others will specialise in jewellery; pieces of gold are passed around the dirty hands of Armenians with black woollen beards; Jews sniff out the pearls.

She also frequents the sales rooms in the working-class districts where the crowds of those made wealthy by the war pounce on pianos, suits of armour, music boxes, thick woollen Indian rugs, silver- or gold-plated ware, plush armchairs.

Sometimes she sets off to the source, goes to the docks where ships from the Far East unload their merchandise that is sold on the spot, at the warehouse.

But what Clarissa likes best are the sales in the provinces where the entire house is being emptied, after death or distraint, from the wines in the cellar down to the door handles, guided by a very sure instinct for these shipwrecks of life, these forfeited items.

Clarissa does not acquire without qualms. And for each purchase she must have a reason:

"It will make a lovely wedding present; instead of giving something horrible … "

"The children need one … "

"It's not for me, I've been asked to buy it … "

"I let the same thing go last year, today you can't get hold of it anywhere … "

For every happy occasion, Clarissa buys herself a little something, as a memento; for every sad one, she buys herself a little something, so as to forget.

Once I have described Clarissa's love for yesterday's cast-offs, half-opened her cupboards full of collections of old shoes, dolls, marionettes, braided waistcoats rescued from oblivion, formal dress-wear, military uniforms, tawdry stage costumes, glittering old rags, tatters, a whole array of trash that not even a taste for antiques can excuse, I shall still not have clarified fully all that I want to explain.

She laughs as she shows them to me:

"Little objects that are of no possible use!"

Still better. Unimaginable little objects, of no antiquity, never sought after, a primitive child's museum, oddities from lunatic asylums, the collection of a consul rendered anaemic by the tropics. She confesses:

"You know my tastes: broken mechanical toys, burnt milk, steam organs, the smell of priests, black silk corsets with floral patterns and those bouquets of coloured beads made from all the flowers quoted in Shakespeare … "

And I suddenly think of the delirious ravings in *Une saison en enfer*: "I loved the silly pictures, overdoors, decorations, canvases by mountebanks, signboards … "

Stranger still is her liking for sham.

She prefers the imitation to the thing itself. She enjoys the disappointment she experiences and that of others. When she sees the way other women look at her pearls, she is amused at being able to arouse so much bad feeling at so little cost. She loves this paraphrase of the truth, the modern religion of window dressing, and this latent mockery of the fake, nature made ridiculous, shown to be useless or imperfect. Wearing fancy dress is one of her delights. She disguises her clothes, dyes her carpets, bleaches her hair, paints pictures of her cats. She has thousands of objects around her that are used for other purposes than one might imagine, books that open into boxes, pen-holders that are telescopes, chairs that become tables, tables that turn into screens, and also those countless bits of surprise jewellery that we owe to the bad taste of the Italians or the Japanese.

The shabby suburban shops displaying their filigree and costume jewellery fascinate her. She has not the slightest longing for panther skins, but she cannot tear her gaze from this crude imitation, with its black patches painted on red rabbit fur.

She has put some glass fruit, some crystal balls, in large bowls; but she reserves her affection for those fruits that are here—the oranges gleam with a viscous varnish, alongside celluloid berries, in glassy, over-swollen clusters, with small, sickly leaves. She only likes dwarf cedars when they are dead and she can smear their branches with red lacquer and make feather pistils and tinfoil petals grow there.

"I'm contemplating an artificial garden," she says. "It would be in the middle of the park. You would arrive there naturally, as though it were the coolest, shadiest spot, and discover sterilised vegetation. You would lie down on moss of that beautiful green that you only find in dyed moss, warm and dusty to the touch. All around there would be beds of coloured beads, tissue paper flowers, and beneath bushes made from glued bits of material, in a smooth glass pool, the motionless frolicking of gutta-percha carp.

Clarissa has a house in town and a house in the country. Our life is spent dashing from one to the other, like a pendulum; they are shared out unequally during the year; one for the dense, brisk winter months, the other for the limpid months of summer. They are not far apart—in the city, by climbing up to the roof terrace, you can make out the country house, perched on the horizon, at the top of the blue hill that, like the well-defined brim of a bowl, marks the outer limits of London.

The first has a noble, self-satisfied atmosphere. Byron lived there. It maintains its standing and, from the pavement and from above, does its best to keep its alignment. The frontage has a severity of line that, were it not for the thought of the myriad eccentricities it conceals, would be boring.

The second, on the other hand, is small and precious, like a neglected piece of Empire furniture left out in a garden. Sunk into its middle is a circular anteroom crowned by a gallery onto which all the bedroom doors open; so that in the morning, from their beds, guests can hurl apples into the bedroom opposite theirs ...

Apart from her two Persian cats that sleep by the fireside where they look like cinders, Clarissa has few close friends.

"Clarissa, let's talk about your friends, if you wish, my companions."

You are the centre of a whole little world that appears to have its raison d'être solely in you. No more than your trinkets, can we conceive of any other life than the one you impose on us. (For you impose things, Clarissa. You are a tall woman, with decisive actions, a definite face, powerful lungs and an air of authority.)

You do not say:

"What could we do this evening?"

But:

"We're going to the Alhambra, box six."

We are your prisoners. Everything draws us back to you. If we are far away, boredom; if we are walking down your street, everything entices us: the large flat button of the door-bell, pleasant to touch, the noise of our footsteps on the marble of the staircase, the parrot's swear-words, the smell of tracing paper and palette that comes from your boudoir, the cameo on your signet-ring, the mauve veins that encircle your eyes.

None of us has any common bond but you. There is, however, a certain family resemblance between us. We are equally slim and youthful, with bright eyes and red lips. We laugh loudly, knock back our drinks, we never get up before breakfast, we dance farandoles all over the house, but we know how to keep quiet when you play music.

You enjoy bringing us together, paying no heed to staunch friendships, yet you nevertheless detect a different virtue in each one of us and you like him or her because of that—Pamela has mahogany hair, Tom slender wrists, Rafael a pretty face and a talent for playing the banjo; as for me, I go well, you say, with your Chinese drawing room.

Here we are, seated around a table, at Murray's, for our common pleasure, which is hers. Clarissa dominates us all with her height; she has more sparkle than the women, more self-assurance than the men;

the maître d'hôtel naturally goes over to her. We gather around her, happy to be here in this comfortable cellar, in this padded catacomb where pleasure presides. The women in this basement have their nails polished, their faces well painted; you can see their armpits. Couples are dancing, circling around an imaginary axis, wringing out the waltz as if it were a tea towel from which the melody oozes. The men in this basement have their arms in slings, bandaged heads; the Negro music tires them a little, takes them back to the indelible memory of the trench where they fell, of the first glass of water. The waiters, as they serve them, stumble over the crutches that are lying on the floor.

There are others, too, fatter, more florid, drinking Pommery in cider bottles, for it is after ten o'clock— the neutrals. They are Scandinavians, Dutchmen, Americans. They exchange knowing glances and under the tablecloth offer two hundred thousand Mausers which can be delivered straight away by sea off Barcelona, or they take out from their hip pocket samples of all the uniform materials worn by the warring armies. They buy back good-humouredly orders that have been rejected (the Russians will take them for sure), overdue contracts. All the tempests of machine-gun fire that will one day be unleashed on men stem from here. Tom sniggers at this interpretation:

"Very much the latest thing; the very last word," he says. "The last word of the dying."

Then, handing one of them a piece of shrapnel recently removed from his head:

"If this may be of use to you again? ... " We are five, gathered around a small table on which elbows and plates are touching. Pamela remains wrapped up in her ermine coat, silent, her eyes tired from the beam of the footlights, rouge still on her cheeks, looking wretched. Then she eats her bacon and eggs, lights an amber-tipped cigarette and bursts like a camellia out of her coat, which slips down her arms. Narrow shoulders, what Rafael calls "being built like a soda-water bottle". She is sad. She says:

"I can't keep a cook."

Tom, whose left eardrum was burst at La Bassée, raises his hand to his good ear to hear better and, thinking that she is joking, begins to laugh, which creases his shiny cheeks, chapped by the great Flanders winds.

Rafael orders himself a large supper and eats it phlegmatically. His face, that of an eighteen-year-old (although he was decorated in the Boer War), is perfectly calm; he himself is collected amid all the turmoil as he always has been during his life which was and is the most unstable, the most humdrum imaginable. He is stubbornly extravagant. You feel he has no connection with the rest of the world. Without obligations, without cares, without a home, without a bank account, without anything apart from the jewellery he wears. Nothing about him reveals his past—the nights partying in Montmartre or in Rome, the nights gambling in Deauville, the nights dancing in St Moritz, the nights of love in Poland or in Madeira have skimmed over his well-bred face without leaving a trace.

Neither insolent, nor obsequious, he goes through life, indolent as a pet animal, with, like all old Etonians, those somewhat spineless mannerisms of the dandy who does not enjoy working.

Clarissa keeps him near her like a pretty cat; like a cat he expects and receives much respect for the kindness of which he is the object, mitigating the condition of dependency in which he places himself by a show of affected indifference.

Clarissa watches him eat.

From time to time, in between two dances, Louisa comes to sit down with us. She is really beautiful, but it is a beauty that is indigestible; we derive no pleasure from it. She does not radiate and at close range she fades.

Louisa is about to speak, her eyes move slowly (she must have been brought up near a line on which only slow trains went by); her mouth opens. She says:

"I ... "

But Rafael interrupts her. She closes her mouth again, opens her handbag, peers into it as if into the bottom of a well; then: cigarette-case, cigarette-holder, cigarette, cotton thread, lighter; then: powder-puff, rouge; she readjusts her beauty-spot.

She is about to speak; her mouth opens again in the shape of a lozenge; she declares:

"I ... "

She is so surprised that she does not continue. She wipes her mascara. She thinks.

"This war is very boring," she says. "They must get very bored in the trenches. The dentist, too, is very boring. I spent two hours at my dentist's this morning—and so this evening I've got headaches, and how … To think that I've waited twenty years to know what toothache's like. Look, I wanted to have a filling in this one—no this one; the bottom molar … '

But she only receives polite interest. She lacks confidence when she is with us. She sees Clarissa whose expression seems to be saying:

"Will you never understand?"

She gets up and goes and shows her bottom tooth to the Duc d'Orléans who places his finger on it.

It is four o'clock. We climb up to ground level, leaving the heavy cigar smoke, the smell of perfume and foie gras beneath us. Outside, it is still night, in the dark street the lampposts wreathed in shadows cast down a circle of furtive light like that of a dim lantern; the policeman checks the locks; some dustmen are reading the French communiqué in the glimmer of a lamplight.

I suggest a taxi, but Clarissa prefers to return home on foot.

"Take my arm," she says. "I so love the night. Why squander half our precious life in slumber? Why, as children, were we sent to bed so early just because it was nighttime—is it not for children? Used you to get up at night? Tell me!"

"Yes, Clarissa. As soon as my mother had kissed me and tucked me up, I would get out of bed. The open window gave onto the balcony and the street below. This balcony was my delight. I can still feel my bare feet on the lead warmed by the sun that used to linger there till evening; I can still recall the fresh taste of the iron railing which I used to lick; I had planted some nasturtiums in tubs into which some real earth bought in the Cours-la-Reine market had been put for me. From the window next to mine, I could see my father in the shade of the studio. He used to draw standing up, with an easy motion of his fine pale hand, beneath the lamp. A grey and violet July dusk was falling over gentle and languid Paris. The horses were pawing the cobbles in the stables, the concierges were smoking at their doorways, in the soft air, the Eiffel Tower did not yet have its necklace of light waves, but sported an emerald on its forehead, menservants were gulping down their liqueurs in tarts' apartments, and as for the tarts, I used to see them at the end of the street, in muslin dresses, in carriages drawn by rose-coloured horses, making their way up the Champs-Elysées, towards the Arc de Triomphe. The sun was going home to bed at Neuilly; they were dining at the Chalet du Cycle."

Clarissa squeezes my arm, takes my hand.

"That's right," she says, "I'm like you; I've the same blood that, on cold mornings, flows through my veins like warm wine, I'm on edge like you on stormy evenings. We are very like one another."

"Very alike, Clarissa. It's a duet; we are in touch. Our thoughts keep pace with one another. In the street, our gazes alight upon a funny feather on a hat at the same moment, our curiosity upon the same blouse …

"I am going to point out this Frenchman to you, with his medals, whose trousers are unbuttoned, and who is washing his hands with imaginary soap, but you have noticed him some time ago."

You say:

"Frenchmen's faces are like those drawing rooms in which there are too many objects. You discover moustaches, a beard, spectacles, warts, moles with downy hair on them."

And I, feeling upset, reply:

"My dear girl, that fellow's a Belgian."

"You love me a little bit then, Clarissa?"

"Well … it annoys me when you take the phone off the hook or when you go off to Paris."

"I ask for no more."

"And you, do you love me?"

"No, but you are to women what London is to other cities."

"?"

"A city which does not totally satisfy you, but which spoils all the others for you."

You are jealous. Anything in my life that is beyond your reach makes you anxious. You do not permit freedom; you find silence difficult to bear. You are eager to know, and knowing does not satisfy you.

You say:

"Describe your girlfriend to me!"

I answer:

"She has a smooth belly, firm flesh that does not show bite marks, wide-apart breasts."

"Young?"

"Very young—she pulls corks out of bottles with her teeth, sits facing the light, is not necessarily at home, gives of herself freely, does not want to make love every day."

"None of which, in fact, is very nice."

"And therefore we come back to girlfriends who say: 'I like to please', 'you're a child', 'my car can take you home', 'you're uncomfortable, take this cushion', 'because I know you like that … '"

1914

DELPHINE

I RETURNED TO MY ROOMS, my head in a whirl as disorderly as the wind which gusts through stations after an express train has passed. Hurtling along the wall at the top of Queen's College, the blast caused people to thrust numbed fingertips deep inside their pockets. My undergraduate's gown, billowing like a black sail, tugged me backwards by both shoulders. I froze beneath this March gale, making it a point of honour to go out all year round, like my fellow students, wearing pumps, without an overcoat and without a hat. Many a habit had had to be sacrificed since that first night at school, when a French boy of fourteen had been obliged to defend the national nightshirt, made of jaconet with Russian embroidery, in a pillow fight with insulted Anglo-Saxon pyjamas.

The corpses of students that remained in the Dardanelles or at La Bassée could be lined up along the length of three canal locks, and yet even more have returned. The colleges are opening annexes. Oxford is no longer that deserted inner courtyard, traversed at certain times of the day by professors without courses, surreptitious Hindus immersed in spiritualism and touring Canadian soldiers; it is not an eminent cloister as it once was, but an industrious hamlet whose inhabitants return from Greek and Latin as though from field or factory. It is no longer contaminated by elegance and lost time. A son's education, the most onerous of English duties, is undergoing restrictions. The days of the daily Clicquot, of balls at the Clarendon, of Latin essays bought ready-written and of life lived on credit, when it was enough to toss off the name of a respectable college to tradesmen to avoid a bill arriving before the end of the third year summer term, those days now belong to the age of the early Georges, when students ruined themselves by living in style and kept mistresses. That is why, like my colleagues, I was reverting to frugal habits, living by the rule and dining almost every evening in hall, even though I had rooms in town. We gulped down the entremets, a sort of alternating pink and yellow mocha cake, which looked like bacon and tasted of pepsin, followed by a large glass of water. While the dons were saying grace, bread rolls rained down on

Harris, the elderly refectory porter who, on special occasions, brings out his album of celebrities in which one can spot viceroys of India, dukes in gaiters, or even, attired in a braided black velvet jacket, Mr Oscar Wilde, the collector of blue china, who only astonished his age because he remained a Magdalen man all his life and did forced labour instead of paying fines.

I was living off the Banbury Road, an area dotted with cheap cottages where there are as many Wordsworth Houses and Keats Lodges as there are nannies on benches, restraining kisses on a lipless mouth, despite twisted spectacles and the irreparable snapping of celluloid collars. A second-year undergraduate, I had passed, proud of having sworn my oath in Latin, in tails, on the Bible, in the presence of the Vice-Chancellor; of having fallen into the river; and of returning, when such a thing was possible, from London, on the last train, known as the fornicators' train, without falling victim to the university patrol after curfew, and master of all I surveyed because of a feudal custom that allowed me the right to the inside of the pavement and the middle of the river.

In the hallway, beneath the stags' antlers where the gong hangs and the bucolic spectacle of stuffed swifts, I found a letter addressed to me. I climbed two floors to switch on the light of a room strewn with books, saddlery, soda siphons, with, on the walls, a toasting fork, a Dante Gabriel Rossetti and a cock fight in which two gentlemen sporting sideburns and stirrups are urging one bird towards the other with the help of paper cones.

I read this:

> *London, this 13th of March,*
> *St Mary's Convent,*
> *King St,*
> *Leicester Square, WC*

> *Jean.*
> *I have been living in London for a week. It is ten o'clock at night, and I have gone to bed, unable to sleep. I have a room in a convent. I hide my eau de Cologne, a luxury of Delphine's. I have not been allowed to leave my suitcase in the corridor. There is nothing but pictures of my mother all around me; she is still the person who plays the greatest role in my life. Since my husband is dead, where I am is of no*

*importance. I don't know why I am no longer in Touraine.
I caught the boat because of a poster. I am a young woman
on my own. I miss the company of men and women and
am repelled by it at the same time. I am as I was in the
old days, by the banks of the Loire, but with nerves that
are worn out. Now I'm feeling sleepy.*

DELPHINE

Delphine.

The name flickers over the screen of my curtains.
Landscapes merge into one another; one wonders
what distraction has prompted a head to appear along
a road, when suddenly there crystallises all around
it some wooden panelling, a door, a window and a
comfortable middle-class drawing room surrounded
on all sides by a tropical landscape which, a moment beforehand, grew there; the drawing room,
in turn, melted away beneath the force of one of
those cinematographic squalls that visit the humblest
gardens. So it is that my white varnished wooden
mantelpiece, discoloured by anthracite, collapses,
falls apart and dwindles into rosy hillsides in which
I recognise Vouvray; the copper plaque begins to
quiver and in turn diffuses into a powerful flow from

which the Loire rises. I see once more a house with
two wings clinging to a flight of steps, chintz curtains
and a pianola. Delphine caused a spasm of asthmatic
whistling to come from it and treated me to the over-
ture to *The Barber of Seville*; the long, perforated roll
of notes folded in a zig-zag, emitting a rippling noise.
While she played, I would gaze at her hair, the tough,
twisted horsehair that I loved; life has added nothing
to those hours, unless it is that hair should not be allowed to be naturally wavy. Then I took her hand and
thought: "Nothing else matters." The bellows of the
pianola ceased to groan, the notes stopped tumbling
down. I should have liked to remain like that for ever;
but we were serious children; never hearing us laugh,
Delphine's aunt began to worry and before long two
foolish eyes, swimming in the water of her lorgnette,
denied us all privacy.

I was allowed to play with Delphine, who never got
dirty and refused to climb up the ladder to the reser-
voir with me. But her coldness, her intelligence and
"words that were not suitable for her age" displeased
my grandparents.

"Delphine," I heard them say, "is the image of her
mother."

Her mother lives in Toulon with a naval officer. A pallid-looking woman, with pink fingers, Annamese costumes, who never dresses up, and who lets exotic dishes grow cold without touching them; proud of days devoted to a table of specious men, wrinkled and full of maritime disillusions.

Delphine did not live poetically except in dreams. She recounted them to me in detail every day. They always contained water, clear when she felt well, muddy when she was tired. Frequently large cats, too, lynxes and panthers, but very gentle and with silky fur. She climbed up into the trees with them as high as the topmost branches from where she let herself drop down into space. She had a thorough knowledge of the meaning of dreams, and since this surprised me, she confessed that she corresponded with Mme de Thèbes and even showed me letters in which she addressed her informally.

Delphine meant the world to me. A world of more individual inspiration, less concerned with approval than the one to which I belonged.

"Never," she asserted, "shall I be like those women who say no when they mean yes."

She went around full of joy to be trying out words,
to be putting ideas into practice. Every experience was
a delight. No vocabulary struck her as unreasonable,
no conduct deserving of disfavour. Though she never
let herself go, she was aware, nevertheless, of all the
imperfections of that world that stopped at the toll-
gates of Tours and, while she was very fond of me,
she was not blind to my own either. She would have
liked to see me wear spectacles.

I tried to dominate her through the mind. I lent her
Dominique. She handed it back to me solemnly. "It's
beautiful", and then concluded: "You are very sen-
sual." It was true. After meals, there were fiery patches
on my plump cheeks, and my nose picked up some
very common smells. Delphine, on the other hand,
seemed to me to be restrained and private. She was
a girl of her times, with a vast amount of knowledge,
sure judgement; clever, proud of the influence she
exerted, at a time when young men are obliged to live
on credit, thanks to their hypocrisy or the leniency of
older people. Everything that is languorous, rebellious,
fecund and unclean in the human species seemed to
have been apportioned to me. But all I could do was
to improve. She had only to offer life that inscrutable

face, that empty heart, to be immediately condemned by fate, to be troubled and beset on all sides, as soon as she ventured to leave home, by scandals, of which her marriage was not the least.

The war is to blame for all that, of course. And in 1917 there was nothing in Tours to prevent a young middle-class Frenchwoman from marrying a Russian officer in leather boots, who had been pursuing her for two months, when the hospitals were overflowing with strange confessions in every language, the hospital trains were taken over by well-to-do ladies who could not cope with the smell of gangrene, tea stalls were set up around the archbishop's palace and the sides of the roads were decked out with large umbrellas beneath which Annamese would take refuge for their oriental liaisons.

But this is well after the period when Delphine and I used to bicycle along the banks of the Loire as far as Luynes, before dinner.

Areas of flooding stretched out between the municipal poplar trees. Dusk was descending over the chalk cliffs, but it did not dim the artificial sunlight from the mustard fields in bloom. A leaden sky flowed above the river; below, in the fields, mottled cattle were advancing slowly, following their tongues.

Delphine was pedalling against the wind. She was wearing a beret and a blue woollen pullover. From time to time she moistened her lips, dried by the wind. Her face, somewhat sullen in repose or when she was at home, relaxed with the effort, became accessible; reflected in the nickel of the handlebars, it seemed broader even, coarse and bracing. At moments like those, I took heart once more; she freewheeled and willingly allowed herself to be pushed, my hand on the flat of her back. Within sight of Saint-Symphorien, the land was no longer laid waste. There was room only for vegetables, cafés and love affairs. We lay our machines on the bank and went down closer to the water. Amid a riot of clouds, the sun was setting.

With its generous and shallow expanse of water, its poisonous sky, its limestone pitted with caves, Touraine became, for a moment, implacable. For a moment, too, Delphine was mine; I lay my head on her knees, my cheeks chafed by the wool of her skirt. My neck swelled; she put her hand inside my collar, motherly, sensible and exasperated, and said: "You're dripping wet." I kissed her warm hand, puerile and full of earthly passions. Delphine turned sour: "I loathe voluptuous people, I warn you." I did not insist, dreading the way she made me feel ashamed of my pleasure and the fits of anger occasioned by my disappointment. The first to get to her feet, she seemed endowed with extraordinary energy. I followed her.

I awoke one Sunday, at about two in the afternoon, in a Turkish bath in Jermyn Street, after a brief sleep broken up by nightmares, hoarse, eyes burning, back aching. I had gone to bed at dawn, after the annual Putney to Mortlake race, in which the Cambridge eight had passed the winning post after having found sufficient lift-off at the end of their blue oars to make up that three-length lead, the memory of which would remain unbearable to Oxford for a year. The two crews had begun again in the evening, a liquid and fraternal contest at the Trocadero dining rooms, then, transported in yelling clusters upon the roofs of taxis, had run the gamut of music-halls; the Empire first, where the affronted boxes exchanged, as though in couplets, college war cries; then the Oxford, where the French show permitted improprieties; then the

Chelsea Palace, where there was a set battle, broken up by the police; on the stroke of midnight, London had in fact become an incandescent mass, ravaged by pleasures, where buses, festooned with advertisements, passed by making swishing noises, where the houses buckled like our indestructible shirt-fronts; portable harmonicas bathed souls in the water of psalms. The electrical sun in the lobby of the Savoy had subsided into the Thames; under cover of darkness the furtive flowers of underground nightclubs flourished: Boum-Boum, the Lotus, Hawaii, where, upon catching sight of us, the disabled porter discovered a pink curtain behind which the face of a Galician Jew, swathed in powdered ochre, dressed in tails with cornelian buttons, drew from a book with counterfoils the tickets for admission to the cellar.

I got up, had a massage and set off for Delphine's.

On the edge of that nebula of dust, of electric gold, of whistles and cries that is Leicester Square, the French convent consisted of three adjoining houses with a pale brick frontage, revealed by the pointed arch of its chapel door on which was written in French *Dames du Bon Accueil*. Sunk into the barred hatch window of the convent door next to it was the bloodshot

eye of the duty sister, wearing a dubious headdress.
I found myself in a parlour, the drawing room of a
middle-class God, where, on a deep-laid wooden
floor, woven esparto water lilies slumbered opposite
green rep chairs.

Delphine entered, dressed in mourning, the oval of
her face accentuated by a strip of white crêpe. I had
not seen her for five years. We embraced.

"Your cheeks are a little less hard as they used to
be," I said, out of affection.

Her face, as smooth as a porcelain bowl, receded
at the sides in an equal curve, drawing up to the sur-
face two dark eyes, liquid and flat, but my memory
hesitated at the sight of a softened mouth, tired at
the corners and which bore her even teeth without
any pleasure. Her nostrils were more flared, and
being elongated, no longer formed part of the line
of her very delicate nose, hooked and slender as to
be almost transparent, the one relief in the mask.
Her expression, too, had changed, more taciturn,
rarely embellished by her former eloquence or self-
assurance. The joy in seeing one another again was
non-existent.

"I'm not taking the veil," she said with a laugh, "but I need rest and this convent had been recommended to me and suits me. God provides us with many a pitfall after misfortune, in order to punish us," she added.

I saw her bedroom, just as basic as those in the gloomy furnished lodgings in the neighbourhood. The walls were covered in old nursery paper, blue with gold stars. Some lilies were soaking in the cracked washbasin. Delphine was getting dressed to go to vespers; I agreed to accompany her.

The sash window decapitated a segment of the square streaked with telephone wires which propped up the immediate weight of a sightless sky. The oriental domes of the Alhambra, the shabby Restaurant Cavour with its dark Chianti stains on the tablecloths, cheered up the image of Sunday with their southern protestations.

In the street she took my arm and traces soon appeared of our former camaraderie.

"I'm glad to be here," she said, "the English are strange creatures, with hands pitted in freckles, who cry at the sight of squirrels and sweet peas. They talk in a garrulous way like southerners without lips, are victims of their nerves and have no resistance to emotions when they happen to feel them. They are all like Miss Mabel, my governess in Tours, deferential and distracted at the same time. She had a prestigious pocket watch inside which was an elegant miniature. In the early days she believed her husband was in love with her. You never knew my husband? He looked like Michel Strogoff, in the first act, when he still has his fine uniform and all his eyelashes; like a tenor whom I had seen in *Hernani*. That's why when I met him for the first time, I turned round. For two months he followed us. He wrote me letters on a paper alternately red and violet. I was thrilled. He asked to marry me. I made up my own mind to refuse. Once I was in his presence I was overcome with panic and two weeks later we were married. You know how he was killed outside Odessa, shortly afterwards. I have not forgotten him; he was good, boisterous and mad like all Russians. Each time I was in the wrong he would weep and beg my forgiveness as he brought out his revolver. I would have been very happy with him."

Delphine describes to me what her widowhood has been. Like a long, fruitless vigil in which, meticulously, she tried initially to detect signs of hope in herself.

"Leaving me alone and keeping me company," she would say, "are the two worst favours anyone can do for me."

Then, treacherously, she spent weeks in Paris in a similar state of anxiety, among different circles, in search of what she termed a system for living, or for not disappearing. She found little there apart from brief reprieves, in which her time was divided among creatures without radiance, bereft of any intelligence or atrophied by a hideous pursuit of pleasure. She refused their mediation.

I certainly recognised the same bravery as before in Delphine, but I perceived a lesser degree of resistance and, with every word, more vehement oscillations. I am no longer much accustomed to young women of my age, having paid only brief visits to France for exams in the course of recent years. Are they all like Delphine? The elder ones had always struck me as abysses of devotion, some dedicated to their duties, those who preferred pleasure imposing on themselves responsibilities no less onerous; all of them ultimately mindful of obligations, loving life and not in the least rebellious against the obstacles it offered them. Delphine, on the other hand, does not parade her selfishness as a disgrace; she treats it as a highly intelligent lesson, as a precise and respected concept that nonetheless exhausts her. She acknowledges her hard-heartedness, which is not the same as it was six years ago, but which was probably being primed then, with such independence that I refrain from thinking badly of her. I reckon that far from finding reasons for persevering, Delphine is waiting impatiently to destroy herself, which lends her a tolerable and fleeting grandeur.

By way of colonial offices shaped like waxen fruits, we reach Westminster Cathedral, which is some way away from the frenetic traffic that connects Victoria Station to the Thames; there I recognised the sanctuary of the new Catholic faith that had reached out over Anglican lawns at the end of the last century. The great British cardinals, Manning and Vaughan, demanded this testimony of piety and good taste, thanks to which prayer would be possible in a modern building. One could indeed rejoice at the sight of these honest, bare basilica walls, all in brick, although Delphine anxiously pointed out a darker line half way up, marking the imminent floodtide of a covering of all too precious marble beneath it, and modern mosaics above.

In front of the sanctuary, framed obliquely in the beams of a pale and fragmented sunlight, a gigantic Byzantine cross blocked the apse. A darkness, in which incense mingled with the fog from outside, shrouded the domes punctured by timorous windows. In spite of the array of chandeliers that resembled oriental headdresses, formed of layers of iron rings from which hung lights on chains, the cathedral was a massive monument and a public utility, like a Roman aqueduct or a railway station. Vespers was being said in the chapel of the Holy Sacrament; the organ was concocting great architectures of sound. On the other side of the brass railings some of the faithful were immersed in contemplation, two nurses, a City man kneeling in front of his top hat, a Chelsea pensioner in red uniform, an Indian Army officer in a turban; three priests were officiating on the altar. Her face in her hands, Delphine was silent. Then she turned to me, an equivocal look in her eyes, and gripped my arm.

"Why am I such a bad person?" she said. "Why do I like everything that's bad?"

Having revealed her thoughts to me in this way, she then smiled.

"You are a very small someone to whom I can't explain anything."

She led me over to the side chapels where the same propensity towards an art anxious to avoid pomp and archaism was manifest. We passed St Patrick's chapel, with its covering of Irish marble and the reredos encrusted in mother-of-pearl shamrocks. All the stones of the world, from Numidia, from Thessaly, from Norway, were beginning to pave the church in mercantile luxury. A black-and-white altar, reminiscent of an actress's bathroom, the fruit of donations from great transatlantic banks, appeared to be reserved for South American devotions. A woman was kneeling on the first step, wrapped in a homespun cape with large pleats that resembled both a monk's habit and a raglan coat. I leant forwards and saw, beneath a hood, a little girl's face with make-up on, swathed in curly grey hair. Her forefinger, encumbered with a large emerald cabochon, was telling the beads of a rosary. I was about to draw Delphine's attention to this Castilian visitor from the time of the Incas, when the lady turned round, and, recognising my friend, greeted her with three hurried and breathless words, uttered in a contralto voice.

Thus did I make the acquaintance of Pepita Warford, an Englishwoman of Cuban extraction, patroness of the convent where Delphine resided. She came up to us, kissed her, spoke to us about the Holy Virgin, about the breeding of marmosets and the advantages of nocturnal life. Delphine laughed, affectionate and excited.

Despite my lack of concentration, I could not but take note of this unusual episode. The moment I set eyes on Mrs Warford, feelings of unimaginable hostility welled up in me, far less resoluble than the spontaneously aroused antipathy we may feel for all those called upon to play a part in the lives of our friends. She had the effect on me that a deceptive vegetable might have that you suddenly discovered was enveloping you. Her piety had the air of culpable ingenuity and when she chirped invective or praise in any language, one was also reminded of a worn-out nightingale.

I was on the point of dissuading Delphine from allowing herself to be destroyed by such relationships. I sensed that they could lead her, via holy paths, towards some disturbing abnegations. Then, I reflected, while Mrs Warford withdrew into prayer once more, that harm never comes to anyone and that to misuse things is an essential condition for mastering them later on. Besides, danger is worth the price you pay for it. So I controlled my ill-humour and did not allow myself any display of harsh wisdom, fearing that I would incur on the part of my friend a degree of anger which I hoped, for her greater good, would soon be turned against herself.

I resumed my studies at the University. I did not belong to any club and I played no games. Adulterated champagne, dry cigars, and the cost they incurred had distanced me from the cliques where Russian princes and the sons of Australians and German landowners set the tone. No less did I fear the bookish brains from Balliol, the Yankees from St John's and the would-be scholars from Worcester or Wadham.

I received some letters from Delphine. They exhibited a poignant desire to have fun. Whether sorrowful or cheery, they brought with them from London a strange flavour of recalcitrance, that touch of precision and premeditated boldness that is peculiar to the French and can seem like excessive politeness. I enjoyed rereading them while working in the Bodleian Library, a sort of barn in which the six centuries-old beams, like the sound post of a violin, registered the slightest noise, while on shelves resembling a fruiterers' displays, fragrant manuscripts lay drying.

One Sunday evening, as I was leaving my rooms to go and dine, I came across Fraser, a fellow of All Souls, whose poet's vanity led him fairly frequently to Chelsea on a Saturday evening. He took me to dine at his college's high table, and, while a Master, violet-veined from the second course onwards, having lined up in front of him wines in cut-glass decanters, passed the port around the table, I learnt that Fraser had made Delphine's acquaintance in London the previous evening.

"She entered," he said pompously, selecting affected words from that outmoded 1880 vocabulary that is no longer used except in university circles, "a public dance hall in the low district of Hammersmith. There is exceptional jazz there and for sixpence you can hire your male or female dancing partner. She appeared hung in black crêpe like a humorous catafalque, as if grieving in repentance, an Anactoria bearing the languor of each waltz like a new sin, flanked on one side by my friend Father W … (he mentioned the name of a Jesuit who had made a name for himself as a comic preacher) and on the other by a strange elderly Spanish child who enveloped her ill-defined features in a panther skin.

"She asked me whether I knew you and we talked about you. After the dance we all went to have breakfast at her home. We really did have a very good time, but she followed us with a sort of sinister pleasure, her eyes aflame and her mouth ashen. Her bruised and precocious heart appealed to me.

"'*Heart bruised with loss and eaten through with shame.*' One day I'll read to you what I have written about that."

And so Delphine, in a few weeks, had gone from the prayer stool to noisy revelry. I was not in the least irritated. Besides, I could not impose my own prejudices to the point of picking a quarrel with her. I did not yet know how quickly certain things are possible in London which Paris will always be unaware of as long as people live there side by side, divided by disdain or fear of the unusual. London is a furtive hermitage which those who have experienced it find hard to relinquish. The streets alone are filled with throngs, with cries, with advertising, with snobbishness, with commercial or sporting feats; they do not encroach upon the sweet open spaces where pleasure seems less perishable than elsewhere. And thus, I explained to myself, Delphine had moved from despair to pastimes that appeared to be going from bad to worse. "What will happen to this childhood friend?" I kept asking myself, without being able to create anything other than a false bond, as superficial as a relationship. "Why am I such a bad person?" I thought again of these words of Delphine's as being the confession of a creature overwhelmed by mere consequences and who is unaware of the origins of the dispute in which she is the unreliable wager. Her childish despotism, that discipline she instigated around her, her revulsion for everything that was easy and likely to become a pleasure, could these be explained by the fear she had of herself?

"I don't feel well," she wrote to me; "the moment I'm no longer having fun, I fret to the point of fury. I waste my energy to such a degree that I'll soon have to think of writing nothing but death announcements. But who is there to say goodbye to? A funerary summer mist and the whole city heated like an oven plate and my ignominy and your disapproval which I sense, is that spleen or what the Abbé Prévost called the 'English vapours'? The sun looks as if it is shining through smoked glass, my food tastes of phenol, I can't sleep any more, and only at night do I find brief moments of coolness, in the parks, or thanks to the powder, well mixed with borax alas, from a little pharmacy in the Commercial Road … "

June had come. The university students, dressed in white flannel, were devouring a false summer consisting of icy sunshine, unkempt greenery and too much water. Doctors in mortarboards passed by along the river, preceded by a boat with a brass band on board. Families, hailing from surrounding areas, on coaches, offered each other sugar from one top deck to another; drapery shop assistants brought out end-of-the-year dress suits and did their best not to feather their oars, not to bump their boats, to show good manners and to call each other "Mister".

At the sight of their sons, the war-profiteers took
their revenge on a back-shop childhood and came
down from the north in nickel-plated cars with the
face of a footman in each headlight. Worn out by
provinces that had their fill, the actor Benson arrived
with his Shakespearean troupe, his wretched watery
scenery, his torn and wobbling fortresses, and we
endured thirty-five acts in one week, by subscription.
The sides of the roads were adorned with picnics, with
irises, with injured motorcycles. The countryside had
become a green desert in which peasants in jackets
and bowler hats paraded. No hollow, limed apple tree
could avoid bending over the cloud-dappled water,
the wake of a boat and the smell of a spirit lamp; the
hay-fever of phonographs broke out from among the
reeds, restoring to nature the poetry which, in order
to succeed, they had borrowed from her. A full liquid
fair now held court until the end of the summer term,
ushering in as at the finish of a race, with encouraging
cries, amid a noise of rattles, fire-crackers, rag-time
and a smell of insipid lemonade and cut-price tea,
the end of the academic year.

There was a nocturnal fête over Mesopotamia.
The college jetties formed brightly lit shapes, half

of which vibrated. Corks popped into the river, rockets became tangled in aqueducts, Bengal lights diffused a creamy layer striated by the water. Alone, I drove my canoe and its cushions damp with dew towards the locks. Searchlights streamed directly over the warm obscurity of the layers of electricity ensnaring Islington church where black ivy and boats that sang drooled. One of them appeared, as though through a suddenly opened door, in the path of the beam. I remained in the darkness, alongside it, and I recognised Delphine, all white, the jet of light full in her face, who was smoking. She seemed drunk and appeared to be gently drifting away. Mrs Warford was also at the bottom of the boat, from where her grey, frizzy hair, which enabled me to recognise her, emerged. In the bow, his feet above the water, playing the banjo, perched an individual of doubtful aspect whom I took for an Italian Yankee. Between his gorilla-like jaws, he held a lighted Chinese lantern, which illuminated from below a Charlie Chaplin moustache and two black nostrils. The night engulfed them again all of a sudden. I saw Delphine throw overboard a lighted cigarette which sputtered.

I was confused and troubled as though I had been done a wrong. Not because I had, with my own eyes, glimpsed in Delphine this new persona that I had foreseen, defiled and prey to deformed people, but because she had concealed her presence from me in a place where I considered myself to be at home. Shortly afterwards, I received a letter from her that did not mention she had left London. My friendship regarded this as a deception, then, reckoning that she may no longer be free, became alarmed. I felt sorry to see a once perfect creature surrendering herself to this abandon, ready to rejoin the sinister herd of lone women, sustained by affairs, one of those whom a vague but imperious calling distances both from the love of self which rescues beautiful women and from the natural attachments which satisfy the others.

It was the very displeasure that this incident caused me, or the interest I suddenly took, despite my mood, in Delphine that led me one month later, at the end of the academic year, to the Ebury Street studio whose address Fraser had given me.

It was reached through a disused cemetery beneath whose lush grass, inert, large Anglo-Saxon skeletons, not deformed by death, continued to live. Outside the garages, the cars being washed filled with freshness a street already lightened by its curtains, its brasses, its red doors, its mirror and 'panorama-ball' merchants, and its glazed paper manufacturers. In the windows of estate agents, photographs eroded by the light provided rustic scenes of bungalows, of bushy trees, of spacious lawns.

I had to knock a long time, even though noise could be heard behind the door. Then Delphine's voice. There was a jingle of keys and chains and the door half-opened onto a pale, puffy face, in which the nose was prominent; the eyelids seemed too short for the eyes. I was so taken aback, that a friendly joke about the way she bolted herself in like an octogenarian failed to pass my lips.

"So, it's you," she said, looking at me without surprise.

Passively, she let me come in.

More than anything else, her expression had changed. Set in a look of fearful stupor, it only came to life to quiver beneath my gaze, refusing to meet it and take it to the core of a heart that one assumed was rotten like a fruit. Following Delphine, I made my way into the studio where a livid light completely divested a woman with greasy, discoloured, almost tomato-red hair, with a bent back, enveloped in shantung, with stockings half pulled up and old slippers. Her rolled up sleeve revealed an arm scattered with pink, blue or black patches. She anticipated my reproaches.

"I've been very ill. I had boils, and then I was blind for twenty-four hours last week. They're hatching plots against me … "

Delphine looks at herself in the mirror, pulls at her cheeks, rubs her forehead.

"I look like an ecchymosis towards the fourth day."

"In the old days you always refused to be a victim."

"I can no longer remember the old days, it's funny, for some time now I've completely lost my memory."

Her sentences faltered. She could see in my eyes that I clearly thought her mad. Pulling herself together, she made an effort to choose her words.

"It's a strange thing," she said, "to be in a milieu. You don't know how it starts, although afterwards, you have the impression that it was planned beforehand, through mysterious forces. You're taken somewhere, you come back the next day and it's a magic circle that snaps shut. You live in the intimacy of people you don't know and whom you would never have chosen. It's a time when you have a great deal of fun, when companionship, a general good mood, the exchange of life forces, turn the group into a useful entity for which you gradually neglect, on a variety of pretexts, everything that is not a part of it. Then, cracks appear. The less good elements seem naturally to gain the upper hand. You are bound together by repulsion, by enmities, not to mention affection. In the end, you want, if not to withdraw, then at least to put some space between yourself and the others. There isn't time. A contact is born, absolute, tacit. You want to fight on your own, to travel, to enjoy yourself; but the group is there, watching; by way of injunctions, circumstances, it finds you again, waits for you at home, recaptures you; everything outside of it seems unacceptable, out of reach. You don't communicate any more except among the initiated, through strange words which are a language. All of this would still be nothing if one day, under the influence of dangerous or more hardened elements, which one imagines stem from other groups that are now dispersed, you did not arrive at a complete revision of the facts of consciousness, at a calling into question of everything, to the verge of nothingness."

"But who brought you to this?"

"Like everywhere else, I've been involved with decent people and with some very bad people, the former led by the latter. And then, it's so odd here … in Paris, there are limits. In London, you have no bearings."

"But what about me?" I said, moving closer to her, "Am I not here to help you?"

She was not listening, exhausted by the effort she had made to think, to speak.

"Come with me, Delphine, I can't leave you like this. I'm going back to Paris tomorrow; would you like me to book you a ticket?"

"I won't be able to."

"Steel yourself."

"I can't anymore."

She sneezed, her mucous membranes swollen, her eyelids red.

"Leave me alone. I need neither your advice nor your criticism. I won't tolerate that from anyone.

DELPHINE

Besides, everything you to say to me is tainted with selfishness and spite. You'd do better to let me rest. Every day, at the same time, I have a temperature. Don't examine those bottles like that; it's none of your business. Have you come here to spy on me? Don't expect to make enquiries of the servants. None of them was willing to stay with me … "

She listens.

"Do you hear that nibbling sound? It's the mice again; I'm infested."

She sees me looking incredulous.

"I'm a sick woman, am I not? Do you take pleasure in humiliating me now that I have let myself go, that I have dyed hair, dirty nails and look coarse? It's a steep decline, I'm well aware. You have observed the regression while taking care not to intervene; from now on I beg you not to involve yourself at all. Have you not aroused my avidity sufficiently in the past? Nowadays I obey a system of loose living; I feel at ease there. Your superior manner annoys me. Go away."

"My dear Delphine, calm yourself. I am not pitiless, I assure you. Let's try to find a way out of all this together."

She weakens, lays her forehead on my hand and suffers excessively. Her joints crack; she claws her nails into the palms of her hands.

I detach myself from where she is lying, get to my feet and search for reasons for her to resist, for excuses.

"Everything that happens to me," she says, "is due to pride."

I was expecting this dreadful word which all women have on their lips and by which they define their humility.

Delphine had arranged to meet me in Regent's Park. I had been to check in my luggage beforehand, for the train leaves for France in one hour. All around me the park, worn away by the drilling of recruits over five years, is recovering again. A soldier in peacetime uniform walks by, glowing like a red pepper in a jar of pickles. Dropped by an invisible squirrel, a nut falls from branch to branch and breaks open on the ground.

I cannot say that the visit to Ebury Street the previous day has upset me. Rather, it has offended me. Delphine was suffering, discontented, attached to her misfortune, prey to a disconcerting vulgarity. Then she came out with words from a cheap novel, and a fainting fit managed to ruin everything. But as soon as I was on my own, the rigorous, resolute image of earlier days returned to me, out of which, reproduced as if on a tracing, the recollection of her recent disorder still grimaced from time to time. It pained me. Not that Delphine's happiness was precious to me, but it grieved me to see this character, whom neither pleasure nor misfortune had managed to destroy until now, so weighed down. I had reckoned her to be incapable of changing for the better, but also resistant to contagion. Her proud integrity had often been intolerable to me, but no less tiresome was this sudden appropriation of her whole being by a pointless destiny.

I then experienced an upheaval of feelings, and thought only of devoting myself to her. All night I wore myself out with worry, and ardently I longed for the joy of rescuing her. Overwhelmed with emotion, I almost got up and went to wake her …

Time goes by, Delphine does not come. London no longer gives back what is given to it. Like a loose net, it receives and retains everything. There are, in this gamut of houses, many creatures like her, who are not living there because of a grief or specific pleasures, but who do not know how to leave. Without chewing them up, between neat quays, London swallows up in its marine oesophagus all the products of the globe which, continuously, remain there when the ships' toil is ended.

She won't come. In the zoo nearby, the roaring of the lions makes the reinforced concrete caverns quiver. Macaws gash the evening with their cries. I remain alone with a heart full of charity.

AURORA

T HE WINDOW OPENS onto a courtyard, where morning has not yet reached the far end. Above me, the worn sheet of the sky, studded with stars, with splashes of acid already in the east. Atrocious morning for an execution. The courtyard is an echoless in-draught. It is too narrow for a dull silence—this one is vertical, as in drainpipes.

Beneath the ground, the apprentice bakers let the heavy dough flop down again, each time for the last time.

I do not want to live here any longer, I'm choking; sleep would be possible were it not for the dreams and the overwhelming weariness of waking up; it is even more impossible to live far from one's friends than with them. I gnaw at my nails, I pull out my hair, I have some successes; but I do not kill time, I wound it.

I should like to go away on my own, with my chequebook hung round my neck in a small metal box; with my suitcase. My suitcase whose smooth flanks are like cheeks, over which all the winds have blown, all fingers have passed; labels from hotels and stations; multi-coloured chalk marks from the customs; and the worn-out bottom that is turning blue with sweat, sea water, vomit, and red where the bottles of eau de cologne have broken inside. Unfortunately, I can no more escape from this city than from myself. There still remains the walk beneath the covered courtyard, the docile pastures of Upper Tooting, the suburban omnibuses, the parks that are as inappropriate as a flower-pot on the balcony, and, behind the Opera house, the aroma of agricultural labours, beneath the colonnade, in the midst of the market that perfumes Beecham's art with a smell of cabbage …

Behind me, I can hear people enjoying themselves. Is there not one among them willing to forsake their entertainment, in order to follow this portent whose interpretation appears to be required of me this morning? Who may also wish to leave? Or, at least, share my sorrow at not leaving? Or console me for the anonymous farce of creation? An advertisement in the newspapers perhaps?

I turn round—it is a woman in an orange tunic tied with a gold cord; arms bare, tanned, very long. Tattooed bracelets. It is Aurora. I recognise her from having seen her dance in the rain at the open-air theatre at Bagatelle one evening in spring. And then there are the illustrated covers of the *Tatler*. "Aurora feeds her pumas." "We walk badly, how Aurora places her feet." On her forefinger, alas, a black diamond, from the Burlington Arcade.

In spite of that, she is attractive. She speaks simply, as if accustomed to controlling her breathing, with measured words. Here she is at the centre of a circle of young men—she has their slimness, their narrow hips, their short hair, their small head; her eyes are level with theirs.

She herself would say: "Women are odalisques with legs that are too short; when they confront a man, their eyes are level with his lips, he looks straight into their bosom—is that seemly?"

Aurora has no bosom and deprives us of furtive pleasures, but of those alone.

This evening there are a few society ladies. Aurora loses all her self-assurance in their presence; she does not like their expressions, conceals her bare feet in their golden sandals beneath her tunic and, pinning her brooch higher, reduces the opening of her neckline.

All the other women, on the other hand, approach her with confidence, kiss her hands, lay their pretty, made-up faces, looking like sweets, upon her shoulder and tell her smutty stories involving generals, theatre directors, servants, suicides, cocaine dealers. Meanwhile, Roger, seated at the piano, his back heaving, plays *Parsifal*.

I am sleepy. The weariness is such that it is restful just to stay where you are and say you are weary. The conversation is lumbering. I go to the dining room. A few dried-up sandwiches are left on the plates, shrivelled at the corners like postage stamps not properly licked, cigarette ash, corks; the level of the liquids is going down in the bottles; the beards of the guests are growing again implacably. Their hands are sticky and their faces ache.

I return to my window. The street is now bluish, steely cold. Beneath the roof, in a tube shaped like an S, a woman sews at her machine, trying to stop the fraying of the night with a hem.

I feel a pointed chin digging into my shoulder. I feel a breast swelling against my back, inhaling the air of the new day which the leaves in the parks has washed at last and sent back with their own fragrance.

"What a life!" Aurora says.

"What a life!" I reply, but I am not really aware of what I am saying. I no longer have the strength to think about who we are, why we are there, whether I like Aurora or dislike her; I no longer care about modulating my voice, my welcome, no longer care about bothering to be charming, about opening my eyes.

Aurora says:

"Whose house are we in?"

"I don't know ... brought by friends ... tepid, sweet champagne ... get away ... where's the door?"

"Ah!" cries Aurora with passion—"to live simply, logically, in harmony with one's self and with the world, the equilibrium of the Greeks, the joy ... "

At these foolish words I pull myself together. Here in my nerve-ends is the strength my muscles deny me; exasperation awakens me. I want to ask her why she goes out dolled up like this, why she camps out like a gypsy instead of living under a roof, like everyone else; I want to crush her perfect feet in their gold sandals with my heel, to wring her neck. I think of fairground manoeuvres under the eye of the police, in the rain, of wretched circus entertainers, I spew up Helvetic heresies and visions of art. Nothing will soothe me other than shaming her, humiliating her.

"Can you do the splits?"

"Of course."

She sets out two chairs and starts to split herself in two.

It is too much. I hurl myself at her so as to strangle her. I squeeze her powerful neck with all my strength, but, with a smile, she clenches her muscles so firmly from chin to shoulders, that, gasping for breath, I have to let go.

She laughs. I am furious.

"Let's go," I say, "I'll take you back."

Aurora climbs into the taxi as if she were mounting a chariot. The vehicle advances silently. Aurora sits in the shadow, her legs crossed, holding her chin.

Calmed down, I have kindly thoughts: "In fact, she has simplified herself extraordinarily. Neither lies nor bombast issue from her slender lips, nor anxiety from her eyes, nor pointless gestures from her hands. She controls her body with lucidity like a precision instrument with powerful and delicate movements on which the strains that crush us are shattered, where, even at this hour, the organs function smoothly."

I envy her harmonious perfection, her inner life free of conflict, her joints free of arthritis, her feet free of corns, her back free of stiffness.

Were I to ask her: "What is to prevent you from behaving badly when you want to, since you are certain you won't have a bad headache the next day?" she would reply: "My personal hygiene."

Suddenly Aurora burst out:

"Don't leave me alone! not alone!"

Sobs.

They contort this body with its hard muscles and violently convulse it. I try to take her fingers, their sinews protruding like steel threads, but they are riveted to her eyes, to her forehead, domed and hard like armour-plating. Warm tears drop onto my hands, which I try to make gentle, but whose gentleness is of no avail. I leave Aurora to herself.

She weeps.

She is trying to live simply, that is all.

Aurora lives near the river. First there is wasteland, then a street of workers' cottages where a gramophone still drones behind a red blind. An iron gate, a paved passage lined with fruit trees. An unusual scene in the early hours.

Aurora strikes a match. Here I am in a room where there are trunks, crates on which can be read in black letters—*TOP, BOTTOM, P&O CABIN*. On the floor, in piles, some books. On a low bed, without sheets, some sable furs and a broom.

From there, we reach a studio. The darkness is pierced by four specks of light—Aurora lets four gas butterflies with blue bodies burst forth from them, one after another. At the first two, the walls draw closer, consolidate their masses, and reveal the layout of the room.

At the other two, the darkness that remained in the corners disappears, rises up to the ceiling where the eye pursues it. Along the entire height of the twenty-foot walls extend arches in relief, supporting windows.

Aurora pokes the fire in the stove. Its glow spreads over the wooden floor and settles in a distant mirror.

The room is bare. Here and there, on pedestals, ancient casts with a waxy patina. At the back, a raised platform.

It is the hearing chamber of a law court not used since the end of George IV's reign. There are still inscriptions above the doors—PUBLIC ENTRANCE, DEFENDANT, CROWN PROSECUTOR, ATTORNEY-GENERAL. Below the judge's dais, the local Apollo; at his feet, a mechanical piano. No other furniture apart from two sofas, the jury box, some African footstools, some fabrics with geometric patterns from the Zambesi.

"This is my house," says Aurora. "It's a trunk, really. I've nothing else in the world apart from these plaster-casts, my dresses and my guns. I once had a large house in Portman Square, with furniture, guests and servants who passed things around on trays. I'm not possessive, I've kept nothing. I'm poor. I've gradually detached myself from all the bonds that the things we love impose on us, for their beauty, their value or the memories we attach to them."

"And now?"

"Now I am on my own in life, sitting on crates, face to face with myself."

"You are as beautiful as another man's wife, Aurora. Is it true you don't belong to anyone?"

"No one must come into my life."

"Do you love your body?"

"It's a storeroom that is consigned to me. I don't put foul thoughts or food that is unclean into it, I look after it, I respect it, I dress it simply … I'm thirsty."

From the floor, by the wall, she picks up a bottle of Australian burgundy, Chambertin Big-Tree, and takes a swig.

Once again Aurora got on my nerves:

"You're probably a reformist, a vegetarian, a eurhythmist, a teetotaller? I loathe this defiance of good manners, this puritan and pagan readjustment of society."

"You're mistaken, there's nothing systematic about me; I'm a Canadian girl who's fond of the simple life."

"Since when?"

"Always. I don't remember having danced or held a gun for the first time … but tonight, for the first time, I feel weary. Gina dragged me off after the theatre to the place where we met. I'm sorry. I'm very weary. I look at the distance I still have to cover, as bad runners do, and I hesitate. Theatrical displays eat up my vitality. You saw me in the car … I am weak, nervous … and you're witnessing all that … It's weird … "

Morning sleep will restore her. But she begs me not to leave her alone, to come upstairs with her, saying that she is going to take a bath.

I am learning about the simple life.

Above the door of the little staircase—LORD CHIEF JUSTICE'S ROBING-ROOM. We go in—it is the bathroom.

She cries out:

"Into the water, Aurora! … "

She undresses in the most natural way, gets into the water, soaps herself, lets the water flow over her body. Perfect body. The muscles in her back ripple like balls of ivory beneath her taut, tanned skin, a substance that is both sturdy and priceless, like the silk used for air-balloons; they can be deciphered as easily as on an anatomy chart, where they cover our organs with pink arborescences; arched loins where the water streams, protruding breasts and, shorn of all heaviness through dancing, long legs, elongated at the ankles, hollowed out on the inside of the thighs, swollen at the supple junction of the knees.

PAUL MORAND

"Come on, Aurora! Out of the water!"

She talks to herself like this, just as she talks to her clothes, to objects. (A habit, she explains, common to all lonely people who spend months without seeing their fellow creatures and for whom the human voice is necessary, as the tuning-fork for all other sounds.)

She pats herself dry, rubbing her face unceremoniously until it turns blood-red. No powder, no make-up, no perfume.

"Why are you laughing?"

"For the first time," I say, "I am laughing when I think of a corset, a detachable collar or boots with buttons … "

In the room there is a pleasant smell of washed flesh, soap, alcohol, steam. Aurora pulls open the chest of drawers where ribbons and scarves are laid out in colours, as if in a prism—she puts on a crêpe-de-chine veil and goes downstairs to the studio again.

The gas butterflies return to their cocoons. Aurora wraps herself in woollen blankets, stretches out on a mattress laid out on the floor. Then she makes sure

114

that her revolver is under the bolster. Her arms and her bare shoulders jut out from the improvised bed. You can see her straight nose in the midst of tousled hair. You can see her eyes. Then you see them no more.

I leave the studio and set off to have a coffee in the cab drivers' shelter.

I went back to Aurora's.

My work completed, I was making my way to the area by the river where the North Sea breeze was driving the smoke clouds towards the west, and beating back the seagulls and the smell of exposed mudflats towards the City. The roads that led me were barely made up and pitted with puddles, and already had a smell of the fields, a promise of countryside.

"You must come out of town with me," Aurora said. "I shall teach you to live as we savages do. In the time you need to have lunch in the restaurant, we shall be naked in a river or else we shall go for a run in the woods. On summer nights I shall take you to sleep in the open air on Oliver's roof terrace, from where you can see the Crystal Palace, gleaming in the distance like a carbuncle in the moonlight. You'll feel

115

much better, you won't have any more headaches, your hair will stop falling out and you'll stop desiring your friends' mistresses, as Frenchmen do."

The taxi pulls up in the middle of the road, as though it had broken down. But the driver does not blaspheme, does not open his bonnet. He opens the door for me—I have arrived. I had promised to be in Epping Forest at seven o'clock, here I am.

It is a September evening, slightly chilly. The giant beech trees do not appear to weigh heavily on the fresh, springy earth, nor do their shadows, or the human toil (though does the toil of English farmers weigh heavily?). On the river the gramophones have ceased crackling. The deer are grazing in the dawn mist.

Aurora had promised to be here at seven o'clock. But she probably sets her path by the sun and will use this cloudy weather, just as her sisters would a traffic jam, as an excuse for being late. Suddenly the branches crackle beneath the lightest of weights, like that of a doe. I turn round—here is Aurora. She runs towards me and her tunic clings to her body like those of the Victories. She holds an attaché case in her hand. She runs on tiptoes, in even strides, well balanced with the motion of her hips. At thirty paces from me, she slows down. Her face, which was merely a clear disc, takes shape, divided in two horizontal parts by her prominent cheekbones, enhanced by a short, mobile nose, like a police dog's. Her momentum gradually relaxes and by the time she reaches me, she is walking. She lays her bag on the ground, then both hands on my arm.

"I'm glad you've come."

"How long have you been here, Aurora?"

"Since yesterday evening. I slept out in the open. On leaving the theatre, Gina drove me here and left me. I climbed up to the Hollow Oak; stretched out on the grass, I ate apples; I could see London between the branches. This morning, I went down to the village, from where I telephoned you."

"This outfit, Aurora, you're going to get yourself arrested."

"The forest warden is a friend. I imagine you'll get undressed too?"

I refuse to. She takes me by the hand, leads me over to a hut covered in dried oak branches. Squatting in front of me, she rekindles the fire, lays the frying pan between two stones and cooks bacon and eggs. I am not used to seeing her like this, her knees black with earth, her hands oily, dirty and unadorned, her tunic pulled up, revealing to the rosy sunlight polished, muscular thighs, those exquisite recesses that a long family inheritance had made so secret and so desirable to me.

I have to give in to Aurora and I take off my socks, my collar. At a glance from her, I relinquish my braces. And here I am undressed in turn with, on my neck, the red mark from my stiff collar, on my legs, the blue mark from my suspenders, blinded by the acrid smoke of the fresh herbs, and like a general in a kepi, stripped by the Touaregs, naked, but still wearing his crown of oak leaves.

Wood pigeons dart through the sky. Aurora takes my stick, aims at them, fires twice, but the birds continue, in a hurry to arrive at Nelson's column before nightfall.

"I was born in Canada," Aurora says, "on the lakes. The men there use coloured flies to catch large salmon, which two men carry back between them having passed a stick through the gills. Women give of themselves freely upon beds of white heather. I became poor very young with all that a fortune used up within a few years is worth to us in experience and pleasure. My parents are both dead. They came from Westmoreland originally. My mother had been very beautiful. I scarcely knew her. She had the smallest foot in the world (I could not fit even a toe into any of her shoes). She had black hair and the complexion of a heroine from *The Keepsake*.

> *"Like waves on a lake came her hair*
> *To die on the strand of her brow,*

"Wordsworth has written. When she came to London for the season, she broke every heart. But she loved my father. She followed him to Canada when he decided to live there. She spent most of her life in bed and died young.

"I get my feelings for the wild from my father. He used to allow me to climb trees, and cliffs from the top of which I took gulls' eggs, and from the bottom, sea-shells. I always went with him when he went hunting. From my earliest childhood he put me on a horse. I followed him like a dog. And my education was really that of a hunting dog. I learned to judge cities from their smell, people by their footsteps, to know which way the wind is blowing, to retrieve game from the most difficult places, and in midwinter I would wade into the water up to my waist to search for the ducks he shot and that fell into the lakes. I can still see him waiting on the shore with his checked trousers, his velvet cap with flaps and his duck-shooting gun; he smiled into his white beard."

I am very cold, but I want to stay here this evening. I have discarded the man-about town; the simple life is good and beautiful; I am giving up my room in Mayfair and the steaming bath that is being run for me at this moment and my fresh, starched shirt that awaits me, unfolded, on the bed. I am relinquishing the benefits of clothes with padded shoulders, of sleek hair, of witty conversation. I do not care about a salary at the end of the month, a pension in my later years, I have no further needs, I expect nothing from anyone, social upheavals do not frighten me and I despise working people who need cinemas and drinks. All I own are the two hundred and eight pieces of my skeleton. I am on a level with the earth, the first to benefit from the magnetic currents in the ground; I am the one burning all the oxygen in the air. It is

Aurora whom I shall rely on to look after me, to think healthily and to live according to the law of nature.

"Good night, child," she says. "May God watch over you!"

She leaves me to this nocturnal journey as if it were a perilous enterprise from which we may not return. Already, I can hear trumpets sounding. The pure air anaesthetises me; I am sleeping beneath the sky for the first time in my life.

I have acquired a sore throat from sleeping out in the open. Aurora is making me herbal teas by the fire, in the studio. Then she says:

"I arrived in India in the autumn of 1909, sailing from Aden. One autumn morning, on a tin-plate sea over which our speed had been cut to twelve knots, Bombay turned its brick façade towards me. Like a silk canopy, the sky stretched out above the factory chimneys, to the right, and to the left, the Elephanta rocks. The trail of smoke in the sky altered less than did the wake from the propellers in the water.

"I stayed on the peninsula for six weeks. I yearned for solitude, for treks in the dry air, which were not satisfied by remaining on low-lying land. The rivers were like corrosive swamps for me, and the ports were dreadfully depressing. I loathe suffocating valleys where there are only small creatures to hunt. I resolved to set off for Kashmir, then Tibet. Leaving Srinagar, I arrived in a country of high lakes, planted with fir trees. The higher we climbed, the lower the temperature dropped. The natives, overcome with torpor, slept as they walked. I had to whip them to wake them up. Cutting out steps in the ice, we continued to climb … "

Aurora points to the studio window from where night was about to fall, for a few all too brief hours. Then her hand took mine once more. Why should it have need of mine, this hand which cuts steps in the ice, which bends pennies as if they were marshmallow? Here are her feet that have only ever worn sandals, that have trod the burning snow, the red sand of Somaliland and scattered the underground palaces of ants in Gabon which, at night, spend their time sawing the earth in two.

Over her body has passed ice, salt, rain, mud, sweat, showers, perfumes. Iron, lead, stone have inscribed wounds on it. In my hands I hold her round head, hard as a paving stone and her thick hair does not deaden the touch. Incomparable caress over the short, bushy hair, which, layered initially by the scissors, ends abruptly on the neck shorn by the clippers. I burnish my fingers on her granite forehead, then on her cheekbones that protrude like pebbles. While she talks, I amuse myself by moving her arms and legs about. The muscles fluctuate silently.

Aurora is covered in scars. One by one I point them out to her and she explains. Here, trampled by a buffalo in Rhodesia; there, in Carolina, a dangerous double jump with her horse, beneath which she was left as if for dead. This hole in her head, a fall at the Olympia, at the bottom of a trap door.

So many accidents and so few adventures. Such a lot of shipwrecks and so great a love of ships, of departures, of all of life if life is movement. No habits—just a few cooking recipes, a few tips on hygiene. A courage acquired from meals without meat, from rooms without heating. So much goodness; silent, practical goodness; basic teaching that I had never been given, that you won't find written down anywhere. Finally, an organic gaiety that never changes, drawn from the oxygen in the air and reproduced all around, the kind of gaiety that endears one more than vice, snobbery or love. A soul cleansed like the body, like the barrels of a gun; helpful hands, a generous heart, a transformer of energy; sweet fruit of the earth, product of my quest, precious beast momentarily captured, Aurora …

Aurora has rented a shed in Dulwich where she has deposited her saddlery and her hunting and fishing equipment. She also has a few wild beasts' heads at a taxidermist's shop in Covent Garden. But her real wealth, her guns, they are at Kent's.

They are shapeless things, wrapped up in old cloths, makeshift bandages for steel damaged by oxidation. But as Aurora unwinds the strips, the weapon appears gleaming and primed. Aurora places on her index finger, in perfect balance, a Holland and Holland sixteen-bore rifle. The barrel is blue. The screws, loosened, inactive, can be turned by the fingernail. The gun, with a duplex-choke, is shaped initially in a rounded horse-pistol butt from which the straight barrel emerges. Carried beneath its heavy belly, like pointed eggs, are the reinforced bullets.

"This is my favourite—a Wollaston ten-bore, for big game," says Aurora. "It came from Major X's sale … This gun's a pal, a real pal. We kill hippopotamuses like rabbits."

And she runs her hand over the hammerless rifle from backsight to butt.

Hippopotamuses, your monstrous innards steaming in the mud of the deltas, crocodiles with your small, round bellies soft as lettuces, hamadryads sitting on your cheeks, brown bears, the pads of your paws more delectable than honey, hyenas like bags stuffed with bones, all of you who died by Aurora's hand, victims of the ten-bore, am I going to fall in love with her?

No. Things turned out differently.

That evening, which was the last, had nevertheless started well. We had dined, Aurora and I, at Old Shepherd's, in Glasshouse Street, which I like for its huge tables, its low ceiling, its toasting fork, its cold buffet adorned with daffodils in ginger ale bottles. We were separated from other people by wooden partitions, above which we could catch a glimpse of Sargent's opulent baldness and Roger Fry's mop of hair.

Aurora was explaining to me how she hunted in Abyssinia, in East Africa, in Nigeria. Well-known hunters granted her their company. They were simple people, "strong and silent men", trappers, solitary individuals hunting wholeheartedly, ruggedly, fearlessly, "of the great breed of those who have slogged away through Africa" when ivory was a trade, before it became a sportsman's trophy; these men held their lives into their own hands, with only an old rifle that took a minute to load standing between them and death, man against beast, men who ate what they had killed and who—the excuse for hunting—when they had not killed anything, ate nothing.

Aurora despises the rich young man of today who sets out from Mombasa with sixty bearers for hunting grounds that are easy and healthy.

Aurora's stories made me drowsy. It was past nine o'clock. The nightclub, like an old hulk from the time of Nelson, had already closed its shutters shaped like portholes. We were eating cheese spread and drinking port.

And thus I arrived, with her, in lands that were inaccessible and unhealthy where little by little you have to leave behind you, firstly objects that are of no use, then the bearers suddenly struck down by a mysterious disease, then the friends killed by luminous flies ...

I thought: "Will Aurora abandon me like this one day, in the antipodes, to return on my own, after such extraordinary years, or will she desert me on a bench tomorrow morning? Everything is possible. Deep down I don't much care for extreme adventures."

Another glass of fruity port.

"No, Aurora shall not influence me. She amuses me, nothing more. She will pass and I shall remain all alone slumbering beneath my old Buddha's sallow fat … "

We leave. Aurora suggests the Café Royal. It is the hour for absinth, taken there, ritually, after dinner. Human beings slowly materialise in the acrid smoke of Burmese cheroots, beneath a gilt ceiling, red velvet, and mirrors with a thousand pillars. Artists in khaki, with Polish inflections, are playing dominoes with their mistresses, their sisters. One recognises sour YMCA females, once encountered in exhibitions of woodcuts. Musicians of the "eligible for call-up" school are preparing distant propaganda tours. Jewish special constables, with their armbands and an eye-glass chained to their protruding ears, await the moment to climb up to the searchlights.

Art provides war with only conditional support. While the Royal Academy paints fervently at General Headquarters, the Independents, weighed down with their conscientious objections, concern themselves with the trucks.

Daniel comes to our table.

"Montjoye is giving a supper party this evening. He has asked me to tell you that he's been trying in vain to 'phone you and that he would like you to bring Aurora, whom he would like to get to know."

Montjoye, or rather Aronsohn (old Norman family, says Daniel), is the Chancellor of the Exchequer's private secretary. He has a set, decorated in the Adams style, in Albany, containing still lifes (still, due to a violent death) against a blue background, arm-chairs in black satin painted by Conder, and some of those Coromandel pieces carved with thick leaves for sideboards. He is happy to offer post-theatre drinks .

"I won't go to Montjoye's," Aurora says. "He's an unwholesome man. He exudes a stench of corruption."

"You talk like the Archbishop of Westminster."

"He's been asking me to come to his house for a long time. I've never wanted to go there. Let's call it pure unsociability on my part … "

I shrug my shoulders.

How irritating remarkable human beings are. I know that Aurora will go to Montjoye's. She wants to go there. She will go just as she goes everywhere, when she is invited. Just as she stays in town extolling the virtues of the forests, just as she dines at the Carlton declaring that she likes to cook her food between two stones; just as she goes naked, out of snobbery and shyness; just as she claims to have introduced order into her life which is nothing but incoherence, ineptitude and confusion. What is the point of these rituals if they culminate in the absurd and ephemeral existence of those women one meets on ocean liners, in hotel lobbies, at fund-raising shows, and who, for their part at least, have the merit of naivety, of vice, or of foolishness?

I know, from having often attended them, that Montjoye's parties are not suitable for Aurora, or for any woman one cares about. But she has to go; she will learn for herself that there are not only boars, but boors too.

"I've got a taxi," says Fred. "I'll drop you."

Montjoye himself opens the door to us. His bulk stands out against a yellow curtain in the entrance hall. He opens the door with a mixture of curiosity and fear, as though he were frightened that the interest he shows in one might be punished with a slap. (Whenever he happens to call on me, his words of greeting are always: "I must be going." Then, he hovers in the doorway until I say to him: "Well, close the door." "In front of me or behind me?" he ventures timidly.) He has eyes only for Aurora, takes no notice of Fred and me, and greets our friend familiarly.

"Aurora! You've come, at last."

He takes both her wrists, strokes them, leads her beneath the lantern with black tassels, uncovers her shoulders with that degree of nerve that only he possesses.

"How beautiful you are!"

In the circular drawing room, supper is served for eight. Grünfeld, the Bolsheviks' unofficial agent, the Duchess of Inverness, a Dutchman by the name of Bismark, Gina and several actors.

Montjoye takes Aurora by the arm, laughs at her embarrassment, pours her a drink and seats her next to the duchess. I loathe Montjoye. He is the person who comes to mind when I try to recall how long I have had a horror of people of taste. I cannot describe the irritating minutiae of his home. From the tongs to the doorknobs, from the candelabras with their green candles to the engraved glasses, everything is perfect. On the work table, which has been pushed into a corner of the room so that people can dance, there are a pile of documents: *Credits to the Allies*, *Loans to the Banque de France*, *Special Expenses*. All of the minister's work is there, in a jumble, amid tuberoses and photographs. But with his genius for figures, his work that can be done in an instant, Montjoye will be able to make sense of it all overnight, on his boss's behalf, the day before questions in the House or a conference.

"We can't manage to get you drunk, Aurora. However, promise me you will drink this, which I have prepared specially with you in mind."

Feverishly, he shakes a bottle that contains four compartments for liqueurs and walks over to the fireplace where his strange face, his large head, his grey hair, are lit up.

Fred sits down at the piano. Grünfeld, having discovered some Pushkin in the library, recites—

"Don't believe a word of it," says Montjoye. "He doesn't know Russian."

From behind her lorgnette, the duchess, sitting motionless, appraises each of us with her cold eyes. She has that sterile youthfulness of fifty-year-old American women, exquisite feet, grey hair, teeth of white jade. She is dressed in nurse's uniform with a large ruby cross over her forehead.

Aurora is enjoying herself in a gloomy sort of way. She is accompanying Fred at the piano. I try to get closer to her and to join in myself singing *All Dressed up and Nowhere to Go*, which Hitchcock, who created it and who is dozing in an armchair, professes not to know. Aurora turns away from me moodily. On a corner couch, Montjoye is talking in a low voice with muffled laughter to the duchess.

"Aurora's going to dance," he cries, suddenly jumping to his feet.

And he leads her to the middle of the room.

"Wait, Aurora, I'm going to make a carpet for you, a carpet of flowers, a carpet of pearls, a carpet for your beauty, for your grace … "

He hesitates, no longer knowing what he is saying, demolishes the vases and scatters the flowers on the ground.

Everything spins round. Everything still spins round in my memory, and Grünfeld's red beard and Montjoye's pale features, and Aurora, especially Aurora, scantily clad, between four lotus-shaped lanterns, her arms outstretched, streaming with sweat, as if possessed, making mad leaps from one end of the room to the other, twirling round with machine-like speed, impressing on our retinas something resembling a Hindu image, with multiple legs and arms. She falls to the ground. Montjoye kneels down beside her, wipes her brow with his handkerchief. He bends over her to inhale her, his eyes closed. I can see the vein in the middle of his forehead bulging, his neck bursting out from under his collar. His head moves closer and closer, then draws back; then, unable to control himself any longer, Montjoye places his lips on Aurora. Aurora shudders, opens her eyes, gets to her feet and, with the speed of a pugilist, sends Montjoye sprawling across to the firedog with a punch to the jaw. Montjoye screams in agony. A bottle of crème de menthe spills its emerald contents over the floor.

"Aurora has created a pogrom," says Fred very calmly from the piano.

I try to intervene.

"Leave me alone, you," says Aurora. "I hate you."

And before any of us could have lifted a finger, she jumps through the window into the little ground-floor garden and disappears.

When I enter her studio, Aurora is sitting on her bed, her chin in her hands, her elbows on her clenched knees. She does not turn her head towards me, I walk straight over to her, in the direction of her eyes, but her gaze goes through me and remains fixed to the wall.

I place my hands on her shoulders: she flinches.

"Leave me. Leave me. I don't want to see you anymore. Go away."

I sit down.

"Go away."

I stand up.

She softens and reaches out her hand to me.

"Sit down. I only wanted to tell you that it would be best to leave me alone from now on. You are of no use to me. I don't want to say more."

She pokes the tip of her umbrella through the straps of her sandals.

"I was beginning to reap the fruits of all my voluntary labour. I am not a nun. I have to both invent the rule and observe it at the same time. And abnegation is not easy for the wild creature I am. You who have not been aware of this long struggle wouldn't be able to understand … Parties like the one last night don't help matters … "

Tears flow down her cheeks. I want to say … But she interrupts me as she gets to her feet and covers herself with a violet veil.

Large zinc clouds jut through the rays of the setting sun. It thunders. Taxis rush madly by.

As soon as we are out of her neighbourhood, people start to look round. Aurora stops, places her hand on mine. Between us this layer of very skimpy veil.

Aurora trembles.

"Will you forgive me, Aurora?"

A vague gesture from Aurora which I interpret:

"It's not your fault."

She waves her hand. The number 19 bus draws up obediently at her feet, by the edge of the pavement. She climbs up to the top deck as if she were walking on a length of unrolled frieze.

The panel states that she can go as far as Islington.

I am very sad. I feel that I shall not really be upset until after dinner.

1916

AFTERWORD

Michel Déon

Paul Morand was thirty-three when Gallimard published *Tendres stocks* (*Tender Shoots*) in 1921, a debut that may seem tardy in these days of untold geniuses of eighteen, and younger. The three novellas that make up this slim book date, in fact, from a few years earlier and we may not be incorrect in thinking that Morand kept them on his back burner, polishing and improving them, precisely in order that they should appear effortless.

Are they, in any case, novellas? No, not really, not in the true sense of the word, and I would feel more inclined to place these first three trial attempts, by a writer who had not yet found his path, among the 'portraits' that he may have considered as an exercise in style, a sort of trial gallop before the future work of his full maturity. Proust was dazzled, as was the high-priest of Surrealism, André Breton, who would later feel disillusioned when his followers supported Moscow.

The astonishment aroused by *Tendres stocks* was huge. Europe was emerging from an appalling war, gathering its breath to overturn the idols of the late nineteenth and early twentieth century. Morand burst forth without warning, accurate, fluent, clever, poetic, cruel. The early years of his life as a diplomat had shunted him between Rome, Madrid and London until he had acquired sufficient know-how to have himself recalled to Paris and to spend the last year of the world war under the command of the most brilliant operator in French politics—Phillipe Berthelot. The names of his friends were Giraudoux, Marcel Proust, Jean Cocteau and, even more so, *le tout-Paris*, including a few ladies of already mature age who held open table at the Ritz, at Meurice's, chez Larue or Maxim's. Here they talked of politics, here they swapped the latest gossip and even the substance of the top-secret government meeting held that very morning. At those luncheons Morand would meet the woman who was to become his wife, Hélène, Princesse Soutzo, half-Greek, half-Romanian, to whom he was deeply unfaithful but whom he would also deeply mourn when she died.

All these fortunate circumstances helped mould a man who was not just someone always in-the-know, but who was also a citizen of the world, an inquisitor, a voyeur and a collector of civilizations. From 1918, once peace was declared, he would parade his curiosity more or less everywhere, resign from the diplomatic service, only to return once more, nevertheless, in 1939, as *Président de la Commission du Blocus* in London, a rather amusing about-turn for a man who, during twenty years of leisure activity between the two wars, had never stopped roaming the planet and bringing home books about 'things seen'—*Rien que la terre, Londres, Bucarest, New York*, not forgetting his writings about China and both the Americas. A compulsive!

There is no reason for what followed to feature in this brief sketch of such a protean figure, apart from the fact that the three portraits etched in *Tendres stocks* herald works of fiction that bided their time impatiently, waiting for peace and the freedom to unleash their creator. Everything is in fermentation, including an unsparing self-portrait, *L'Homme pressé*, in which those who were close to him, as well as his readers, would identify him before the time came for him to bid farewell to everything that he loved, which he did in *Venises* (*Venices*, published in Euan Cameron's translation by Pushkin Press), but also in the profoundly moving *Le Flagellant de Séville* which, regardless of its author, deserves to be ranked among the masterpieces of the twentieth century, as a masterpiece for all time.

Let there be no mistake—Morand was still writing about himself, just as he was in *Tendres stocks*.

2011

PUSHKIN PRESS

Pushkin Press was founded in 1997. Having first rediscovered European classics of the twentieth century, Pushkin now publishes novels, essays, memoirs, children's books, and everything from timeless classics to the urgent and contemporary.

This book is part of the Pushkin Collection of paperbacks, designed to be as satisfying as possible to hold and to enjoy. It is typeset in Monotype Baskerville, based on the transitional English serif typeface designed in the mid-eighteenth century by John Baskerville. It was litho-printed on Munken Premium White Paper and notch-bound by the independently owned printer TJ International in Padstow, Cornwall. The cover, with French flaps, was printed on Conqueror Brilliant White Board. The paper and cover board are both acid-free and approved by the Forest Stewardship Council (FSC).

Pushkin Press publishes the best writing from around the world—great stories, beautifully produced, to be read and read again.